The Streets Are
Paved with Gold

The Streets Are Paved with Gold

by Fran Weissenberg

HARBINGER HOUSE
Tucson · New York

HARBINGER HOUSE, INC.
Tucson, Arizona

Copyright © 1990 by Fran Weissenberg
Manufactured in the United States of America

This book was set in 10/13 Linotronic 300 Aster and
♾ printed on acid-free, archival-quality paper.

Designed by Rebecca Gaver

Library of Congress Cataloging-in-Publication Data

Weissenberg, Fran.
    The streets are paved with gold / by Fran Weissenberg.
        p. cm.
    Summary: The eighth grade is a difficult time of transition
for Deborah, as she attempts to reconcile her desire for a regular
school life and friendships outside the Jewish community with
her strong attachment to her very traditional family.
    ISBN 0-943173-51-5
    [1. Jews — Fiction. 2. Family life — Fiction.] I. Title.
PZ7.W44816St   1990   89-24413
[Fic] — dc20   CIP
                                                            AC

*For my husband and our families who lived it
And for the young ones to know it —
Deborah, Judith, Peter, and my granddaughter
Lauren Frances Roth*

The Streets Are
Paved with Gold

DEAR READER,

I have taken some liberties with places and events from the past for the sake of the story. The characters are fictional.

Debbie Gold's family and other Eastern European Jewish families of the time spoke Yiddish. I've explained Yiddish (and Hebrew) words where they first appear in the story and again in a special glossary at the back of the book.

— FRAN

1

MOST OF THE TIME, my dreams are mixed up or crazy, and forgotten before I wake up. Not this morning! Still smiling, I opened my eyes and could see my breath forming in the cold morning light. Mama was already in the kitchen, shaking down the coal stove.

Klop! Klop!

The sound of the milkman's horse reminded me that David, my older brother, was out in the cold helping Mr. Green deliver milk. Shivering, I snuggled deeper into my feather quilt. I shut my eyes and drifted back into my wonderful dream.

In it, dressed as a Japanese girl in a red kimono, I walked beside Ben Stein. He was also wearing a kimono and had a musical instrument slung over his shoulder. We were strolling through the empty hallway of Jefferson High School, talking excitedly.

In real life, Ben Stein sat next to me in Glee Club, but I could hardly say a word to him without blushing or stammering.

Dreams are great, but odd. For instance, why were we walking in Jefferson High? Was the dream a sign that I was going to be lucky and go to Jefferson in September?

The best part of the dream was the Japanese costumes. A few weeks ago, Miss Beck had announced to the Glee Club that we would be doing a musical play set in Japan. It was called The Mikado. So, did the dream mean that Ben Stein, the cutest boy in the class, and I would be playing the lead parts in the play?

This was a dream I did not want to forget. I decided to record it in my diary. That way, no matter what happened, I'd always have it.

Reaching underneath the bed for the box where I hid my secret things, I poked under the scarf in the corner where the diary usually was. I couldn't find it.

I knew what had happened. That pesky Michael must have taken my diary. I wished I could put my hands on my little brother and shake him hard. He slept with Elliot, his twin, on the other side of the curtain I'd strung up for privacy. Ignoring the icy blast that hit me when I threw back the covers, I dashed around the curtain. There, asleep in the wide bed, were the twins — two black, curly heads, in a tangle of arms and legs.

Which one was Michael? I couldn't tell, and the rising goose bumps on my skin sent me scurrying to pick up my clothes. I fled into Mama's warm kitchen, which was filled with the smell of freshly ground coffee.

Mama, her back straight and hair drawn into a tight knot, was stirring the oatmeal at her shiny black stove. Donny was banging a spoon on his high chair tray. I kissed his neck and sniffed his sweet baby scent.

"Good morning, Mama."

Mama answered in Yiddish. She never spoke English. You'd think she was a greenhorn, an immigrant right off the boat from the Old Country. But Davy was seventeen, so Mama must have been in America for at least eighteen years. Time enough to have learned English. She has promised to go to night school when Donny is grown.

It was on the tip of my tongue to complain about Michael. But I needed Mama to say yes this morning. Mama is a short woman until she says no. Then she becomes six feet tall. Besides, I could handle Michael myself.

"Mama, last night I fell asleep waiting to talk to you."

"I got home after twelve. Mrs. Fein had her baby late."

"Babies sure pick funny hours to be born. What did she have?"

"A boy." Mama's eyes softened. "Mrs. Fein had a hard time and is very weak. I'm going to run upstairs to get her breakfast. I fed Donny, but tell Papa..." There was a worried look on Mama's face. "Tell Papa I'll see him before he goes to work."

She took off her apron and put on her old brown sweater. "Mama," I wailed, buttoning my skirt. "I have to talk to you."

"So what's more important? Should I listen to you or feed a woman who just had a baby?"

"I know what's more important, Mama. After all, I'm almost fourteen."

"So what is it?" Mama's stocky frame was already in the doorway, one foot tapping.

"This afternoon I'll be going to the library with..."

"With Esther."

"No, I am going with Mary Regan."

"Mary Regan." Mama stepped back into the kitchen and closed the door. "Mary Regan. So who is this Mary Regan? From where are her people?"

"I don't know."

"What does her father do?"

"How should I know?"

"Regan? That's a Jewish name?"

"No, Mama!"

"You can't go to the library with a Jewish girl?"

"Yes! No! Oh, Mama!" I tried not to grit my teeth. "It's this way. Miss Lee, our history teacher, picked the two of us to do the report on Patrick Henry. She didn't check our families."

Mama said nothing. Then she shook her head. "If the teacher tells you to go, what can I do? So go."

Mama could get me so mad sometimes, even when she said yes. I couldn't help banging the pots and slamming the dishes. At least it got the boys up. I was ready for Michael when he walked into the kitchen, his hair tousled and in his undershirt.

I grabbed his shoulder and squeezed hard. "Where did you put it?" I hissed. He looked so bewildered I loosened my grip. "Where did you put my diary?"

He opened his mouth and shook his head with a look of injured innocence. "I don't know. Honest, I never touched it. Ask Elliot."

His twin brother had appeared, so I turned to him. "Did he, Elliot, did he take my diary?"

Elliot thought a moment and shook his head. "But yesterday a marble rolled under your bed and Michael went after it. Did you touch the box, Michael?"

"Oh, that's right. I had to lift the box to get the marble. But I swear," he raised his right arm and looked at me sincerely, "honest, I didn't even look in the box."

"I'll check it. Mama is upstairs helping Mrs. Fein and her new baby. I'll get your oatmeal."

While I was stirring the oatmeal, I hummed a tune from *The Mikado*. I must have been dreaming because I dripped oatmeal on the stove and it had sizzled dry. I gave the boys their oatmeal and rushed to clean the stove, Mama's pride and joy. Then I dashed to the bedroom and pulled out the box.

There it was. The diary had slid to the opposite corner. With just a minute to make a fast entry, I grabbed my fountain pen and wrote on the next clean page: "A dream: Ben Stein, Thomas Jefferson High School, and The Mikado."

After I finished dressing and made my bed, I returned to the kitchen. Papa, wearing the shiny, blue work suit that hung on his slight frame, was handing the baby a zwieback biscuit.

"Good morning, Debbie," he said, his blue eyes lighting up. "Hey, you look mad this morning."

"It's Mama. She's such a greenhorn."

"What happened?" Papa helped himself to a roll and butter as I told him about Mary Regan.

He nodded his head. "Don't blame Mama. One thing leads to another."

"Papa, this is America and it is 1922."

"I know, I know." There was a smile on Papa's face. "And only two years ago, women got the right to vote."

"Exactly. How can we be good citizens if we're not allowed to get to know our fellow Americans? Mama insists we have the same old friends."

Papa had turned his attention to getting the twins ready for the long walk to school. There was snow on the ground, so Papa bundled warm scarves around their necks. As he bent to put on their galoshes, he started to cough so hard he had to sit down.

Papa's coughing worried me. Sometimes I heard him in the middle of the night, coughing, coughing.

"Why don't you put on your own galoshes?" I asked my brothers angrily.

"Papa likes to help us," Elliot replied. But they finished fastening the galoshes themselves.

When Papa was all right, I hurried into the bathroom. After splashing icy water on my face and brushing my hair with quick, hard strokes, I peered into the mirror. Two dark, almond-shaped eyes peered back at me. I smiled at myself, pinched some color into my cheeks, and ran out of the apartment.

Outside, the boys were so far ahead I could hardly see them. Esther was hurrying out of her building, a tenement house just like mine, with long rows of garbage cans. This part of Brooklyn was filled with tenements. Esther and I had walked to school together since first grade. She was average height and on the chubby side, with thick, brown hair, and beside her, I was petite with long, black hair.

"Hi, Deb, are you late, too? I was fussing with this coat."

"A new coat! Looks great. Wear it in good health."

"Not exactly new. For a hand-me-down, it's not too bad. Could be a little looser." Esther's dimples showed. "At least the color is good."

"Better than this gruesome, gray hand-me-down. My mother thinks as long as it's large enough it's fine." I tugged at the dead, stiff cloth. "Boy, do I wish I could get a new coat."

"Ask your fairy godmother," Esther suggested.

For some reason, "fairy godmother" made me think of my dream. As we walked, I told Esther about it.

"What a dream!" she said. "My mother thinks dreams can tell the future."

"Really?!"

Esther nodded. "And if only a part of the dream should come true, which would you like it to be?"

"What do you mean?"

"Well, there's being in Jefferson High. And getting to sing the lead in the play. And not least of all," Esther looked slyly at me, "there's that handsome Ben Stein."

"Do I have to choose?"

"I know which one I'd pick." Esther had a serious look. "More than anything I want to go to high school in September. But with my father out of work so much of the time, I don't have a chance. I hear Woolworth's is hiring girls of fourteen. So I guess it's Continuation School for me. What about you?"

"It depends. If there has to be a choice between David and me, it may be David because he's a genius and should go to college. Besides, he's a man and…"

Esther nodded.

"As Uncle Pincus is always saying, 'Men have to earn a living and women…'"

"Women stay home and have babies," Esther finished. "With three brothers, it's the same in my family."

It wasn't funny but we laughed.

"So your first choice would be to go to high school, too?"

I hesitated. "I'm not sure. Right now, more than anything, I want to play Yum-Yum in *The Mikado*, especially if it's opposite Ben Stein."

"Hah, you're a sly one. You get the lead in the play and

you get Ben, too. By the way, what's *The Mikado* about? I never heard of it."

I told Esther that the play took place in Japan. A beautiful young woman, Yum-Yum, is betrothed to marry her guardian, an old man. But she is in love with Nanki-Poo, a traveling musician, who is really the son of the Mikado, the Emperor of Japan. "It's funny and has great music."

"I can't wait to see it. You have a good voice, so is there any reason you won't get to do Yum-Yum?"

"Well, there's Jenny Sharp."

"Oh, the blonde girl with the braids?"

"Yes. And she's always talking about her voice teacher. He thinks Jenny's going to be an opera star."

Ahead of us, we could see the high bridge that spanned the railroad and joined the two neighborhoods — our poor one and the nicer, mostly gentile one. On the other side of the bridge was the red brick school which children from both neighborhoods attended.

"Sounds like real competition," Esther said. "Hope she's not going to keep you from getting what you want."

"I wish I knew. But I did get something Jenny wanted," I said as we reached the street.

"You got Ben."

"Quit kidding. Both Jenny and I wanted to work with Mary Regan on the Patrick Henry report for the citywide contest. Miss Lee picked me. Was Jenny mad!"

"Gee, Debbie, I feel like I'm talking to a future celebrity. If you get the part of Yum-Yum, and then you win the medal for the Patrick Henry contest, you'll be famous."

I laughed. "Too many ifs. By the way, Mary and I are going to the library after school to work on the report. So don't wait for me."

"Hey, the plot thickens. Poor immigrant girl from the wrong side of the bridge is befriended by richest, most popular girl in school," Esther said in her best melodramatic voice.

I giggled. "You ought to write for the stage."

"You recognize my talent?"

"Sure."

"But will the rich new friend come between the immigrant girl and her old but poor friend?" Esther looked at me.

"Hey, come on. Nothing can come between girls who've known each other since they were born." We were almost at the bridge with its long flight of stairs.

"Es," I said as we paused on the first step, "do you remember when we were in first grade, we never had to walk up the steps?"

"Sure, I remember. We'd both stand on the first step. I'd hold on to the right rail and you'd hold on to the left. Nobody could pass us. Then the men who were going to work on the elevated train would come up behind us..."

"And before we could put our two feet on the second step somebody was lifting us to the top!"

We laughed and ran up the stairs past the train station and across the bridge. I stopped for a moment at the top of the stairs to admire the winter scene below. The snow lay in neat, white patches on the rows of brownstone houses and in between the bare trees. A gray church with a large cross loomed just ahead of us. Beyond that, we could see the red brick school.

The school bell clanged just as we reached the school yard and we both sprinted to our class lines. I slipped to the rear of my line, hoping no one would notice me. In front of me and in her right place was Jenny Sharp. She turned around, surprised to see me.

In a loud stage whisper she asked, "How come you're at the wrong end of the line, Deborah Gold?"

I said nothing, hoping to discourage her. Again came the whisper, so loud that Miss Hale, leading the line, whirled around.

"Jenny Sharp! First thing in the morning and you're talking. Put your hand down. I don't want to hear your excuses."

I could see the red creep up the back of Jenny's neck. She muttered something under her breath and managed to give me a dirty look as we walked up the stairs.

2

THE DAY that began with my beautiful dream was turning into a bad one for me. I walked to the lunchroom with butterflies doing tricks in my empty stomach. Why had I agreed to have lunch with Mary Regan? It seemed right earlier this morning when she suggested it. We'd have a chance to plan what we would do in the library later. The trouble was that Mary ate with some of the snootiest girls in school.

I stopped at the table where Esther and Sarah had already unpacked their thick, mouth-watering sandwiches.

"I'm starving. But I promised to eat with Mary Regan."

"Really, Debbie. Some class!" Sarah, the comedian, pushed her glasses up and pointed her nose to the ceiling. With her mouth full of sandwich, she looked funny.

"You mean you're going to eat with those ritzy girls?"

"Sure, I am."

I didn't want my friends to know how unnerved I was, so I walked quickly to the opposite side of the lunchroom. I threaded my way among the crowded tables. I was tempted to turn back, but Mary spotted me and waved.

Lucky for me, it was Assembly Day and girls were required to wear a blue skirt, a white middy blouse, and a red tie. If my skirt wasn't of the best wool, no one knew.

"Here, Debbie, I saved a seat for you next to me." Mary patted the space beside her. "You know the girls."

I greeted Jane Simmons and Millie Ryan, girls I knew only slightly. Jenny Sharp gave me a cold nod. The girls were almost finished with their sandwiches of thin, white bread, cut daintily in half with the crusts removed.

I slipped my hand into the paper bag and groaned silently. My fingers grasped Mama's thick, rye-bread sandwich. It was welded together with globs of delicious chopped liver, and the smell of fried onions seeped out. I pulled my hand out of the bag, empty. As hungry as I was, there was no way I'd be able to eat that sandwich at this table. I couldn't take a chance on biting into it and having it erupt into a mess.

"Onions! Do I smell onions?" Jenny, a pained expression on her face, asked the question as if she couldn't believe it was possible. "Onions make me sick."

Four pairs of eyes focused on me. I could feel the heat in my face. I was thankful when Mary said, "Funny, the smell of fried onions always makes my mouth water."

It was a relief when the conversation changed to what the girls had done on the weekend. I was happy to listen.

"I saw an opera," Jane said, "and it was boring. But my mother insists I go with her." She shook her straight, brown hair in disgust.

"I love the opera," Jenny said. "Signor Perrini thinks I ought to study for the opera and perhaps become a famous singer." Jenny's green eyes widened with pride.

"Well, that's a modest statement if I ever heard one," Mary laughed. "As usual, my mother dragged me shopping. But we did get to see 'Abie's Irish Rose.'"

"Is that the Broadway show about a Jewish boy marrying an Irish girl?" Jane asked.

"That's right." Mary turned to me. "Did you see it, Debbie?"

"Not yet," I replied. There wasn't much chance I would because my family usually went to the Jewish Theatre on Second Avenue.

By now the girls had finished their lunches. "Aren't you eating that delicious sandwich?" Jenny asked me.

"I'm not too hungry today," I stammered.

Jenny said nothing, but I could see she didn't believe me. Before I could stop myself, my hand picked up the bag and tossed it into the trash can. It was the first time I had ever thrown good food away, and I was in a state of shock. Mary assumed I was finished and suggested we begin our work. I was grateful to concentrate on our project and forget my stomach.

The afternoon slid by and it wasn't until the last class, Glee Club practice, that I caved in from hunger. Ben Stein was munching a bag of cookies. I was usually too shy to do more than nod, but the terrible hunger pangs and the crunching sounds of the disappearing cookies made me turn to him. "Excuse me, could you spare a cookie?"

Surprised, he held out the bag. "Sure, Debbie, help yourself."

I picked a cookie and, as daintily as possible, took a small bite, then stuffed the rest into my mouth.

"That sure was good."

"Have the bag," he offered, a wide grin on his handsome face.

When Jenny, who sat on the other side of Ben, started her endless conversation, it gave me a chance to push more cookies into my hungry mouth. The bag was almost empty when Miss Beck sounded the chord for quiet.

As usual, Miss Beck had us listen to the catchy melodies she played on the piano. When we sang, our voices filled the auditorium. Then Miss Beck had an announcement.

"The time for deciding who is to play the different roles in The Mikado will be coming up soon. Our principal, Mr. Davis, has said he is willing to sit for the tryouts. Starting today, anyone who wants a chance to practice solo can use the stage or stand by the piano."

An excited buzz filled the room. Walking up to the stage to solo was going to be hard for me. The last time I had tried it, my knees shook so I could hardly be heard.

Ben turned to me. "Are you going to try, Debbie?"

Before I could answer, Jenny was saying, "Mr. Perrini, my teacher, thinks I'll have no trouble getting the lead. Won't it be fun, Ben, to play the lead with you?" Flutter, flutter went the eyelashes over the green eyes.

When Miss Beck called for a volunteer, it was Jenny who raised her hand.

"Good. From the stage or the piano?"

"The stage, Miss Beck."

Jenny, tall and blonde, with the poise of an experienced performer, stood on the stage waiting for Miss Beck's introduction. I had to admire her. She had a quality in her voice that must surely have come from taking lessons.

Jenny was going to be tough competition, I thought, as I walked out to meet Mary. She was waiting for me at the gate. Her soft, tan coat with matching tam on her blonde hair reminded me that Mary was one of the best dressed girls in school.

"Hi, Debbie, are you ready for the trek to the library?"

"It's now or never," I replied.

Mary giggled and I felt better.

We started out in silence, our boots crunching on the snow as we walked. After a few minutes, we turned to each other to speak at just the same moment, then stopped. Again we started and stopped. By now we were laughing, and the ice was broken.

"Would you like a piece of this chocolate bar?" Mary asked.

I accepted eagerly. The talk turned to books, and I was delighted to find that Mary shared my feelings. It wasn't hard to tell her how much the library meant to me.

It was in the second grade that Davy had first brought me to this dignified building with its wide, stone steps. The large, sunlit rooms were filled with shelves of books. I trailed after Miss Williams, the librarian, so much she soon got to know me.

Miss Williams had a rule: if you took out a fiction book, you also had to pick a nonfiction one. I never questioned this. After all, Miss Williams had the magic key to the wonders of the world.

Mary was talking about her father's library.

"You mean your father has a library at home?" I could

hardly believe this. The Gold home had maybe three or four books. Did all Americans have their own libraries? At the risk of reminding Mary that I was from the wrong side of the bridge, I had to know.

"Mary, is it usual for people to have their own libraries?"

"Well, you see, my father is an authority on Shakespeare. That's how he came to accumulate so many books. So now it's a library."

I couldn't hide my amazement.

"Debbie, you will have to visit my father's library and see for yourself."

Did she mean this to be an invitation? I had only a moment to wonder about it before we were mounting the steps to the public library.

Miss Williams greeted us. She was wearing her usual wide, patent-leather belt, starched, white blouse, and straight skirt.

"Why, girls, I had no idea you two knew each other."

After we explained our assignment, she brought us armloads of books on Patrick Henry. For the next two hours, we read, whispered, discussed, and took pages of notes. Through the big window, I could see the setting sun.

"Mary, I really have to go home," I said, stretching my weary arms.

"It looks like we have just about got this report done. I'm glad Miss Lee picked the two of us," Mary yawned. "We work well together."

The pale winter sky was growing dark as I sped happily over the bridge. It felt good to have done so much work on the report. And I had made a new friend.

Up in the night sky, a little star was peeking out. I shut my eyes and whispered, "Starlight, star bright, first star I see tonight..."

And then I paused to consider my wish. To the usual one — that we could be a real American family — I added, "And please let me get the lead in *The Mikado*."

3

IT WAS a late hour for me to be getting home. I was surprised to find Mama scrubbing down the kitchen wall at this time of day.

"Hello, Mama."

"So, it's dark already."

"I know, Mama. But we had so much work to do. I'm sorry."

Mama said nothing. She attacked the wall with her cleaning rag. Was she angry because I had gone to the library with Mary?

At the far end of the dining room table, Michael was getting his Hebrew lesson from Mr. Sugar. Three times a week Mr. Sugar came to prepare the boys for their *bar mitzvah*. By trade a baker, he worked all night. During the day when he wasn't sleeping, he was teaching.

When I tiptoed in, Michael stopped reading to wink at me. Mr. Sugar's eyes were closed and he seemed asleep. Michael, up to his old trick, deliberately skipped a few pages but continued reading in the same monotone, hoping to shorten the lesson. It didn't always work; suddenly Mr. Sugar made a snorting sound and his eyelids flew open.

"No! No skipping!"

Did being caught embarrass Michael? Not a bit. He would try it again and again.

After Mr. Sugar left, Mama handed me an envelope. "Read," she told me. "Read."

Inside was a typed letter from Mr. Davis, the principal of our school. I skimmed down the letter. "Mama, he wants you to come to school tomorrow to see him about Michael and Elliot. What did you two do?" I asked them.

They both shook their curly heads. "Nothing. Right, Elliot?" Michael turned to his twin. The two were identical in almost every detail. Their dark hair curled around their black-eyed faces in the same way.

People were always trying to tell them apart, but the family had no such trouble. Elliot was the quiet one, his nose in a book most of the time. Michael was a human dynamo. In our small flat, he seemed to be everywhere at once. There were no secret places from his prying eyes.

Once I'd written in my diary that Ben Stein was "my Rudolph Valentino." I'd hidden the diary under the bed, but was it safe? Evidently not, because for the next two weeks, Michael followed me around, repeating, "Who is my Valentino? Who is my Valentino?" Can a person be blamed for wanting to throttle such a brother?

Elliot said nothing; he just looked frightened.

"You got a C in conduct on your report card," I reminded Michael.

"So what? I wasn't the only one. Nobody else's mother had to come to school."

"For nothing they tell mothers to come to school?" Mama asked.

Mama cautioned us not to tell Papa about the letter until after supper. She allowed nothing to spoil her good food. So at the supper table, I told them about *The Mikado*.

"Any chance you could get the lead?" David wanted to know.

"Well, I have to compete with Jenny Sharp, who is getting voice lessons. So who knows?"

"What if you don't get the lead, Debbie?" Papa asked. "I'm sure there are other parts."

"But it's nice to be the star," David said. That's David. He's not only a math genius, but also the family musician. He had already organized a band.

"So why don't you take some voice lessons?" Michael asked.

"What's wrong with her voice?" Mama asked. "We don't need opera singers."

"Aunt Becky thinks you could be a singer," Elliot said.

"Aw, everything Debbie does Aunt Becky thinks is the greatest."

I frowned at Michael, although there was some truth to what he said. Aunt Becky, the youngest and gayest of Mama's four sisters, taught me every song I knew in Yiddish and English, starting many years ago when she came to this country and lived with us, as all of Mama's sisters had.

It was Mama's persistence that brought her four sisters to America. That and her diamond ring. To buy a ship's ticket for even one sister, Mama had to pawn her most precious possession — her diamond ring. With that money, the first sister was able to come. She stayed with us until she could earn enough money to redeem the ring. Then Mama pawned it again for the second sister to come over, and so on until the ring had brought all four sisters — Sadie, Rose, Yetta, and Rebecca — to America.

Of my four aunts, Aunt Becky was my favorite. Next week was her birthday and I was planning to get her a gift.

"Mama, is the pushcart street a good place to shop for a birthday present for Aunt Becky?"

Mama nodded. "I'm going tomorrow after school. You come with me."

"How come you're going so late in the day?" Papa asked. So Mama told him she would have to go to school. She handed Papa the letter.

"What does this mean, boys?"

They shrugged their shoulders. "Honest, Papa, Elliot and I don't know."

Papa shook his head and looked worried. "Debbie, you will have to go to the principal's office with Mama."

"Me, Papa? You mean I'll have to translate Mama's Yiddish?" A big knot started growing in my stomach.

I turned to David. "Wouldn't it look better if an older person came with Mama?" I pleaded.

He understood my embarrassment. "I'm sorry. Tomorrow is an important test in mathematics." He ran his fingers through his hair.

Who could blame a mathematics genius with big plans for college next year? But I was desperate. I knew what Papa was going to say even before I asked him if he could go with Mama.

"How can I afford to lose wages?" was his expected reply. "Besides, we may be deciding tomorrow about whether we will go on strike." He shook his head.

So I was it. I tried to untie some of the knots in my stomach by reminding myself that there were other mothers around who could not speak English, but it didn't help much. My sleep was filled with nightmares, and I woke up feeling groggy. Before I left for school, I gave Mama directions on where to meet me.

"And, Mama, put on your good black dress," I told her.

"Do I look crazy? I have to go shopping at the pushcarts with my good black dress on?"

"Mama, please wear the black dress. I have to leave now. Please, Mama."

All that day I was so nervous about Mama and the meeting with Mr. Davis that I know I must have fouled up my math test. And I needed to give math my utmost because it was my worst subject. When your older brother is a mathematics genius, teachers have a queer way of looking at you if you can't walk in his shoes.

In history, I volunteered to identify the Battle of Bunker Hill and pointed to a spot on the map that caused Miss Lee to smile. "That state hadn't even been settled yet, Deborah."

It was Jenny Sharp who walked confidently to the map and located the right spot. I was worried that Mama would come to school dressed for shopping. If she did, I'd be looking for some hole to drop into.

When the bell rang, I hurried to meet Mama, but I was

caught in a jam of boys and girls. Over their shoulders I glimpsed Mama standing under the clock, like a strange island in the crowded hallway. She was wearing her shabby brown coat and some of the students were staring at her.

Mama, relieved to see me, started talking in loud Yiddish over the din in the hallway. I heard Jenny Sharp's laughter and turned around. There she was with two of her friends, her eyes darting over Mama, not missing a thing.

"Mama, why don't you take your coat off? It's really hot in school," I whispered to her. I was relieved at how presentable she looked in her good black dress, with her hair combed into a thick bun. It was a short wait before we were ushered into Mr. Davis's office.

Mr. Davis, looking stern, pinched off his rimless glasses. "Why are you here?" he glared, pointing at me with his glasses.

"My mother doesn't speak English," I said, one hair above a whisper.

"She understands it?"

I nodded.

Two brown envelopes, one marked "Elliot" and the other marked "Michael," were on his desk. Mr. Davis pulled out the contents of the envelopes and showed them to us. They were test papers. But what was odd was that the marks on each test were almost the same for each boy.

"Their teacher asked me to look into this matter."

Mama's face had turned a beet red. She was excited and started speaking in a high-pitched voice. When she realized Mr. Davis could not understand her, she turned to me. "Tell him, I'll swear on my life, that my boys are not cheats! Since they were babies, tell him, they always thought alike. They knew the same words and answers."

I turned slowly to Mr. Davis. "My mother says that my brothers are not cheats. From the day they were born, they were identical in everything they did or said. It's hard to believe, but my mother..."

Mr. Davis held up his hand. "Just a moment. There is no

question of cheating since they sit a few rows apart. But there is a problem, and that is why we sent for you."

Mama looked relieved, and Mr. Davis continued. "From their work, we know they are both bright. Yet Elliot hardly ever opens his mouth."

Mama nodded. "Explain to Mr. Davis that Elliot has always been the quiet one. Remember how we worried that Elliot would never talk."

"That's right, Mr. Davis."

"What's right, Deborah? What did your mother say?"

I told him, and he looked thoughtful. "Could it be that Michael speaks for the two of them?"

Mama nodded her agreement.

"Interesting situation," the principal said. "I'd like to meet the boys. Deborah, would you mind asking Miss King to excuse them?"

When I got to their classroom, I saw Michael immediately, frantically waving at me. But where was Elliot? I spotted him two rows over, with his head down.

"Are we bad?" Michael asked, as soon as we walked out of the classroom.

"Mr. Davis said nothing about your conduct. He wants to talk to you about something else. Don't worry," I added, when I saw how pale Elliot had turned.

Mr. Davis shook hands with each boy. "Boys, I'd like you to help me find out something about twins. Is that all right?" They nodded.

"Deborah, why don't you and your mother wait outside, while I ask the boys some questions?"

When we returned a few minutes later, Mr. Davis was smiling. "Incredible. I wouldn't have believed it, but they gave almost the same answers to everything I asked. Even the wrong replies showed similar thinking."

The boys were grinning with relief.

Mr. Davis continued. "Since the boys have this unusual ability, it would be best to have them in separate classes. We'll put this young man in Miss Green's class tomorrow," he said, pointing to Elliot. Mama and I felt this was a mistake. But before we could put our thoughts into words, we'd been ushered out of the office.

Elliot looked worried. "There's such big boys in Miss Green's class."

Michael tried to comfort his twin. "Miss Green is a nice teacher. She doesn't pull ears like Miss King."

It was too late to do anything now. And Mama had given each of us money to buy a *nosh* (a treat) when we went shopping at the pushcart street. I was already thinking about the gift I would be buying for Aunt Becky when we got there.

4

IN A happy, relieved mood, we walked briskly, feeling the icy-cold winter wind. The two boys, frisking ahead on the winter streets, had spotted the sweet-potato man. His small, gray stove on wheels was sending up trickles of warm smoke.

"Mama, our fingers are frozen. Should we buy a hot potato?"

"Get for all of us."

We were chilled and the hot, steaming yam would warm us, especially since we knew the trick of taking little nibbles, passing the potato from hand to hand, and making it last as long as possible. By the last bite, we had turned the corner and entered the noisy excitement of the street. Lined from one end to the other with pushcarts, it was a jumble of colors, of mouth-watering smells, of hawking peddlers and bargaining shoppers.

Mama left us to do her shopping, with instructions to meet at the fish store. With eight pennies each to spend, the boys were prancing, sniffing, touching, and happily chattering about what to buy. I decided to add my dime to the dollar I had taken from my coat fund for Aunt Becky's gift.

I quickly passed pushcarts with mounds of oranges, earthy brown potatoes, and hardy, red winter apples. There were more interesting things ahead. The good-natured crowd jostled me as I tried to look on both sides of the sidewalk. The stores had also set up stands to display their goods.

I passed the chocolate-covered halvah, my favorite candy, and almost stopped. I was tempted, but I might need the dime later. There was a fountain pen for one dollar on the next pushcart. It would be a useful present because Aunt Becky, who had started school as soon as she came to America, was going to graduate this year. No, it wasn't quite right; I decided to look for something more personal.

I passed the stands of household goods, pots, pans, and an assortment of dishes. At one pushcart, I spotted a pretty camisole in a pile of underwear. It cost too much, so I had to put it back.

There had to be something I liked for the right amount. Ahead, the boys were waiting for me at the pickle man.

"Didn't you buy anything yet?" they asked, their faces smeared with chocolate. "We had chocolate-covered halvah. And boy, was that good. What did you get?"

"Nothing yet. I'm saving my dime." But the smell of the pickles in the barrel of brine was too much. "Gosh, would I love a pickle."

They cost two for a nickel. Should I spend it? But the boys had put their heads and their money together. They handed five pennies to the pickle man, who wore a heavy sweater with one sleeve rolled up, revealing an arm white with brine. He plunged this arm into the deep barrel and came up with two dripping pickles. I got a generous piece from each of my brothers.

We spotted Mama leaving the chicken market, carrying a bag of freshly killed and plucked fowl.

"Better hurry," Michael said. "Mama is going to the fish store where we have to meet her. We'll help you look."

At the notion pushcart, I spotted a grass basket under the piles of threads, needles, and shoelaces. It was round and woven with sweet grass, and when I held it to my nose, it had a delicate fragrance. I lifted the lid gently and was delighted to find a checked gingham lining. It was perfect.

"Mister, how much does this cost?"

"One dollar and a quarter."

"We still have five pennies left," the boys cried.

"Will you take one dollar and fifteen cents for it?" I was elated when the merchant agreed, because it was just right for Aunt Becky.

We got to the fish store just as Mama was emerging, loaded with packages. Michael got to carry the live carp, wrapped in newspaper, that would be slipped into the bathtub as soon as we got home; then Mama would prepare it for our Sabbath dinner.

Mama would kosher the chickens and meat she'd bought, after she'd soaked them in cold water for an hour. I liked to watch Mama's hand dip into the salt box and rain heavy kosher salt on the meat resting on the drainboard.

Once I asked Mama why Jewish people had to kosher their meat. She explained that Jewish people are not allowed to eat the blood of another being. Koshering with salt ensures that there will be no blood left.

As soon as the packages were put away and Donny was brought down from the neighbor, Mama gave orders. "This Sunday, special company is coming. The house has to shine."

"Who's coming?" we all wanted to know.

"Uncle Pincus is bringing a friend — a rich man — to meet Becky." Mama shook her head, convinced that her sister, who was twenty-three and still not married, was going to be an old maid. "If only she would like him."

I was so delighted at the idea of a rich suitor for Aunt Becky that I decided to start cleaning immediately. First, the bathroom. I rushed in with my pail and brushes, but the sight of the black carp swimming in the bathtub stopped me cold, because I knew he'd be part of the *gefilte fish* Mama would make tomorrow. Unlike the twins, I avoided the carp as much as possible. I decided tomorrow would be soon enough to clean the bathroom, when the black carp would be no more.

I couldn't wait for Sunday. It wasn't only that the rich suitor was coming, but there was a puzzling question I needed to ask Aunt Becky. She had loaned me a book of poems. On the front page in bold handwriting was "To my best student, Becky. With all my love, John O'Neill."

Aunt Becky had never mentioned John O'Neill. Who was he? And why was it signed with *all his love?*

5

IN THE GOLD FAMILY, you didn't have to look at the calendar to know which day of the week it was. If you woke up to the smell of simmering cabbage soup, it had to be Sunday.

Why the same menu week in and week out? When we asked Mama, she would shrug her shoulders. "So I know who is coming?"

"Mama," I asked once, "why don't you ask people to call you on the telephone in the candy store to let you know if they're coming?"

"Well, by the time I get to the store to answer the telephone, I am half dead worrying about why they're calling." Mama shook her head. "This way is better."

"This way" meant that any of Mama's sisters and their families, or Papa's relatives, or any friends, might just drop in anytime on Sunday. There was always enough food for everybody.

"This way" meant a huge pot filled with cabbage and other vegetables, meaty bones, and chunks of beef simmering for hours on the stove. Next to it was an equally large pot filled with potatoes boiling in their skins.

Anyone who was hungry got a bowl of steaming soup in which to plunk the skinned white potatoes. Along with the crunchy pumpernickel, there was a choice of each *tante's* (aunt's) specialty: *strudel, latkes, ruggeles,* and *blintzes.*

It was fun to answer the knock on the door. Who was there, and what were they bringing? When would Uncle

Pincus's friend arrive? The house was spic and span by the time the first knock sounded. Michael flew to open the door for Aunt Yetta and Uncle Pincus.

Short, with a paunchy stomach around which was proudly draped his gold watch and chain, Mama's brother-in-law Pincus was the family capitalist. He always gave each child some money, usually pennies.

Michael grumbled to Mama many times, "How come if he is so rich, he only gives pennies?"

"From him you could learn how to respect a penny," she would answer.

But this morning Uncle Pincus had to be more generous. Aunt Yetta was wearing a diamond brooch pinned to her dress. When she hugged Michael to her large bosom, the pin scratched him. Never one to miss an opportunity, Michael let out such a howl that Uncle Pincus dug into his pocket and pulled out nickels and dimes. So we all profited.

My favorite cousin, Annie, just one month older than I was, arrived next. I was really glad to see her, especially since her family was moving to Buffalo soon. With Uncle Pincus's help, they were planning to open a women's clothing store there.

"Annie, I have so much to tell you and we have so much to do. Where should we go?"

"The usual place."

The "usual place" was cross-legged on my bed with the curtains drawn tight for privacy. Facing each other, we used to play cards, dominoes, jacks, and other games when we were younger. Now we were writing a book — a novel of romance and love. But first I wanted to tell her about *The Mikado* and Ben Stein.

"And if you get the part, you'll be in a real love story. Is Ben Stein tall?" Annie has a thing about tall men. I guess Annie, who is already three inches taller than I am, expects to be tall herself. She is still flat-chested, however, and doesn't have her period yet.

"He's much taller than I am," I assured her.

26

"Let's get down to writing another chapter of our romance!"

"Good idea. Where are we?"

We read what we had written. On the other side of the curtain, there was a loud argument going on. I parted the curtains and poked my head through. The twins and two cousins were having a noisy fight over their Go-Fish game.

"You're not allowed to play on your bed," I told them.

"So what about you?"

We had already posted our "Do Not Disturb — Writers at Work" sign. "Can't you read the sign? Writers at work, it says."

Everybody knew writing was work, so with this there was no arguing. Off they went to find a new place, probably under the dining room table. That reminded me that I had Aunt Becky's book under my bed, and I fished it up to show Annie. After I read aloud the note from the mysterious John O'Neill, I looked at her.

"Doesn't that mean John O'Neill loves Aunt Becky?"

I nodded. "But who is he?"

"And if he loves her, how come we don't know him?"

And then I did what my mother does. "John O'Neill? John O'Neill? Is that a Jewish name?" I laughed.

"Why are you laughing, Debbie? This is serious."

"I know. But I sounded just like my mother."

"Do you think she loves him?"

"I don't know. What about Uncle Pincus's friend? He's rich — and Jewish. Maybe he's here."

We hurried out, hoping that Aunt Becky's secret wouldn't show on our faces. All was confusion and noise, with the men sitting around the dining table, smoking and sampling some of the goodies. They were arguing — that is, my father and Uncle Pincus were disagreeing loudly over something. If Uncle Pincus was the capitalist, then my father, who helped organize the union in his clothing factory, was on the opposite side.

In the kitchen, the tantes were gossiping and catching up

on the week's news. Everyone, nervous that Aunt Becky would be late, expected Uncle Pincus to come rushing into the kitchen, and he did.

"Where is that Becky?" he demanded, shaking his finger at us and looking at his watch.

"Don't worry so much," Aunt Rosie giggled. "She promised to be on time." Aunt Rosie's giggle, always contagious, made us relax.

When the knock sounded, I opened the door hoping to see Aunt Becky. Instead, a small, pink-faced man, wearing a dark coat with a fur collar and holding a big cigar in his mouth, stood there. Uncle Pincus, behind me, stepped forward to greet his friend.

"Come in, Selig. Come in and meet the family."

The visitor removed his bowler hat, revealing a shiny, pink, bald scalp. I shook my head when I looked at Annie. Even after she had mouthed, "rich and Jewish," I still shook my head.

Though he wasn't handsome, Selig Samuels was pleasant. He shook hands solemnly with each of us as we were introduced. Then we all sat around the dining room table, and each of my aunts offered him her specialty. He sampled everything.

"Must be a family of cooks," he said.

Uncle Pincus, trying to hide his impatience, said, "Becky should be here any minute."

There was a silence that seemed to go on and on. Finally my Aunt Sadie tried to fill it with her favorite story. "I have to tell you how these two boys," she pointed to Michael and Elliot, "saved my life."

"Is that so? Such young boys!" Selig remarked.

"That's right — they were even younger then."

It may have been Aunt Sadie's favorite story, but it wasn't Uncle Pincus's. He shook his head, his face red with anger, but nothing could stop Aunt Sadie. She brushed her unruly black hair out of her eyes, pulled out her handkerchief, and began.

"It was 1911 and I was still a greenhorn. It was bad for us. Finally I got a job at the Triangle Shirtwaist Company for three dollars a week. You know how many hours I worked at that sewing machine? Sixty hours a week! For such low wages I should have quit, but if I left, there was another greenhorn to take my place. So I stayed until we went on strike."

"So enough of the story already," Uncle Pincus finally had to say.

"Let her finish, Pincus," my father said quietly.

"That was some strike. We got beaten up, and after a few weeks we went back to work. Now it was worse. The bosses were angry at us. They kept the steel door, which led to the toilets outside the building, locked so there wouldn't be an interruption of work."

"That Saturday," Aunt Sadie clasped her hands and shook her head as if she couldn't believe what she was saying, "fire broke out in the factory." She paused to wipe a tear from her eyes. "My friends were trapped and...and they were burned to death or jumped out of the window and were killed." Aunt Sadie was blowing her nose.

"Tell how you were saved," Michael and Elliot prompted.

"You see, my sister Molly was giving birth that day and asked me to help her. So that's why I wasn't in the shop."

"That's the day we were born — March 25, 1911," the twins said so proudly that everybody laughed, even Pincus.

Selig nodded. "The Triangle Shirtwaist fire. I remember it. It wasn't easy for anybody in those days."

"That's right," Uncle Pincus said. "Factories didn't grow on trees either. Did I ever tell you how Yetta and I started our first factory?"

Selig hadn't heard it, but we had, many times. It wasn't Papa's favorite story, but Mama gave him a look, so he said nothing.

"We were both greenhorns and we also worked long hours, not like today." Pincus shot a glance at Papa. "So we had saved a little money."

"That's right," Aunt Yetta agreed. She was my short aunt, and because she was childless she always worked with her husband. "I pawned my engagement ring to get enough money to buy a sewing machine. In those days we used our own flat for the factory. We pulled up an old table for a work bench, and kept the irons hot on the stove in the kitchen so we could press.

"Now we needed some work. So Pincus went to the factories and offered to do it cheap. Remember, Pincus?"

Her husband smiled and took up the story. "Soon we got so busy we needed a helper. One morning, I got up very early and walked to Hester Street. All the people who needed work came there. There was this old man with a sewing machine he carried on his head..."

"Old Sam."

"That's who it was. I bargained with him. He was old, so he came cheap."

"Some worker he was," Aunt Yetta remembered. "He stayed with us until we moved into a real factory. They don't work like that anymore."

Despite Mama's warning look, Papa had to say, "I hope you paid him a decent wage, even if he was an old man."

Before Pincus could start another argument with Papa, Aunt Becky suddenly appeared at the door. All eyes were on her and all conversation forgotten as she apologized for being late. She was a breath of fresh air; her cheeks were glowing from the cold and her blue eyes were sparkling. She hugged and kissed each of us, and soon everybody was laughing, relaxed, and hungry. But first, Becky was introduced to Selig.

We could see he was smitten with her. He smoothed his bald head, fixed his tie, and lit a new cigar, although he was only half finished with his old one. From the moment Becky walked in, his eyes never left her.

All of us were hungry, so Mama fed the children first, and I held the baby while she dished up the soup for the grownups. After we'd all stuffed ourselves, the fun began.

Aunt Becky, who had never taken a music lesson in her life, sat at the piano and accompanied herself as she sang. First it was old Yiddish songs, requested by the older people, then popular American songs.

When David brought out his violin, Mama was bursting with pride. She had good reason for choosing Davy as her favorite. Then it was time to show what I could do, so I played "Für Elise" on the piano.

After the applause, Aunt Becky suggested I sing a solo, and "Alexander's Ragtime Band" was my choice. Then I did one song from *The Mikado*, and everyone assured me I would get the lead in the school production.

Aunt Rosie asked Aunt Becky and me to do an old Yiddish favorite, "Eli, Eli." It's a sad song about suffering; the first time I heard it I cried. We must have done it well because Selig was impressed.

"Very beautiful," he said. "It must be a family of *musikers*. You and Becky are taking lessons?"

Aunt Becky shook her head. "It's too late for me. Debbie should be studying."

"Why does a girl need to study singing?" Uncle Pincus asked. "She's going to become a cantor?"

"Of course not," Aunt Becky said. "But Debbie should be allowed to develop her voice. As a matter of fact, I would like to take Debbie to the Bronx Settlement House, where they have an excellent music department. Of course, if it's all right with my sister."

My heart leaped. "Look out, Jenny Sharp," I thought, "here comes competition."

But my mother said, "The Bronx? Such a trip. We'll see."

I wanted to rush over to Aunt Becky to hug her, but Selig had reached her side. In what he thought was a quiet voice, he asked to see her next Saturday.

Everyone must have heard, for there was a sudden, tense silence.

"I am busy this Saturday." I could hear the silent groaning among the tantes. My mother had an agonized look on her face. I know she was thinking she had a sister who would be an old maid.

"But I am free on Sunday."

There was much relief, as each aunt tried to hurry her sleepy offspring into coats and do all the kissing and shaking of hands before they departed. Soon everybody had gone and only Aunt Becky remained.

I could wait no longer. "Aunt Becky, am I really going to see the music teacher?"

She nodded. "I have a friend who knows him. If your mama agrees, he will make the arrangements."

I wondered if this friend was the mysterious John O'Neill.

"And Debbie, don't forget this Wednesday we're meeting at the Second Avenue Theatre. Jenny Goldstein is the star."

"Thanks, Aunt Becky. Did you ever hear of 'Abie's Irish Rose'?"

Becky nodded. "Maybe we'll see it for your birthday. Anyhow, remember Wednesday."

Before I could assure her that I had no intention of forgetting such an event, the twins were telling Aunt Becky about the birthday gift *we* had bought for her. For their five pennies, which I forgot to return to them, we were now equal givers of this birthday gift.

I saw Aunt Becky's eyes light up when I handed her the basket wrapped in tissue paper. "It's just lovely. Thank you all."

I knew Aunt Becky would understand about the boys, even though I couldn't say anything about the money. That's what's so great about my Aunt Becky.

I also had her book of poems under my arm. "I'm returning this book, Aunt Becky. I read it and enjoyed it. I also read something by John O'Neill on the front page."

Aunt Becky turned pale. She looked into my eyes and shook her head. I knew this was to be kept a secret.

She whispered quickly, "You'll meet him this Wednesday."

6

"ISN'T THIS THE slowest week in history?" I asked Esther and Sarah as we unpacked our lunches.

"I hadn't noticed," Sarah said. "What's the hurry?"

"Big doings on Wednesday." I bit daintily from my sandwich, which had been cut in half. "It's Aunt Becky's birthday."

I told them about my plans to meet Aunt Becky to see Jenny Goldstein in a show in Manhattan. "But the best is that I'm going to meet a mysterious someone."

"Someone? Male or female?"

"A man who is very important in my aunt's life, I think."

"You think?"

So I had to tell the girls about John O'Neill after swearing them to secrecy.

"Wow! That's romantic. But if he's Christian and she's Jewish, will she marry him?"

"There was a story just like that one in the *Bintel Brief* that my mother read to us," Esther remembered.

"What's a Bintel Brief?" Sarah asked.

"It's a column in a Jewish newspaper. People write letters asking for advice," I explained. My mother also read the letters aloud.

"What advice did the Jewish woman get?"

Esther answered: "She should do what she feels she must. But she should also consider that in some families when such a marriage takes place, she could be mourned as if she were dead."

"You mean they sit *shivah* for her?"

Esther nodded. The idea of mourning for my Aunt Becky sent a chill up my spine. But I went on with the happy news.

"That's only part of the story for Wednesday. Aunt Becky thinks I ought to take voice lessons. Her friend John O'Neill is going to introduce me to a voice teacher."

"Wow," said Esther. "Then you'll really show Jenny Sharp!"

I nodded. "Maybe. Now you can see why I can't wait for Wednesday."

"Don't forget to mention it to that dreamy Ben Stein," Esther advised.

"I planned to," I admitted and could feel the heat in my face.

"Hey, the girl is blushing," Sarah teased.

In Glee Club, I actually interrupted Jenny's endless conversation with Ben to say, "Did I tell you, Ben, that I may be studying voice?"

It stopped Jenny dead in the middle of a sentence. Ben turned those heavy black eyelashes to me. His eyes crinkled when he laughed. "Hey, that's great. Imagine, I'll be sitting between two talents."

Jenny wasn't quite buying it. "What's your teacher's name?"

"I'm not exactly sure yet," I spluttered. Maybe I should have kept my mouth shut. "I'll let you know when I find out."

"Do that, Debbie."

They both looked at me as if I should be saying something. Things chased around in my head, but nothing came out of my mouth. I'd better change the subject. I could tell them about Elliot's trouble in his new class. But before I could say, "My brother," Ben had turned back to Jenny's endless conversation. How did they learn to speak so easily? I wondered.

I was glad to start singing, and I did not stop when the class was over. I hummed "Here's a How-de-do" all the way home. Only the sight of Elliot with a bloody nose cut my song short. He had been beaten up by the class bully again.

Mama was wringing her hands, "He doesn't hurt anybody. Why are they hitting him?"

"Don't you remember when I used to come home with a bloody nose every week, Mama?" David asked.

"But it stopped."

"Sure. That's because I learned to fight back."

"Elliot, you can't hit back?"

Elliot, whose nose had stopped bleeding, shook his head. "They're too big for me."

"Michael, you're such a *shtarke*, such a strong boy, why don't you help your brother?"

"It's not my fault. Miss Green's class always gets dismissed before my class."

"The only thing that will help," said David, "is to give Elliot some boxing lessons."

"He'll get hurt," my mother worried.

"He'll get hurt more if he doesn't fight back."

On Wednesday I had to do my homework, press my dress, and finish getting ready before I could meet Aunt Becky. In the other room, Elliot was getting his first boxing lessons.

David made both the twins strip down to their undershirts.

"It's too cold," Mama complained.

"If they're cold, they'll work harder to keep warm," David said. "Now, boys, here's how to put the gloves on."

The gloves, borrowed from a friend, were much too large. They weighed Elliot down and he could hardly lift his hands. For Michael, they seemed fine. He was in his glory, prancing and jabbing with the heavy gloves as if he'd worn them all his life.

"Here's one for you," he said, almost landing one on me as I rushed around trying to get ready.

"Pest!" I muttered.

Poor Elliot. Try as hard as he could, there seemed to be no way for him to ward off Michael's punches.

"Protect yourself. Hold your gloves up in front of your face," David directed.

I couldn't watch and was happy to leave. Mama felt the same way, and she offered to come with me to the train station on the bridge.

"You know how to go and where to get off?"

"Yes, Papa gave me directions last night. Don't worry about tonight, Aunt Becky will come back with me and sleep over."

"Here, take an extra dime, just in case."

"Thanks, Mama."

The elevated train was deserted at this hour, since people had already returned home from work. I didn't mind the empty trains because there was so much to think about. What was John O'Neill like? If they loved each other, would I be old enough to recognize it?

What was love, anyhow? When Ben Stein turns those dark eyes at me or smiles, and my heart pounds, is that love? Once his hand touched my arm and I felt an electric tingle shoot through me. Was that love?

I knew about marriage and children — but maybe not everything. What I didn't understand was, if you meet someone and you think you're in love, how can you know that you want to spend the rest of your life with that person? And what could you talk about for so many years? It was a mystery and I wanted to find the answers.

If Brooklyn was getting ready for bed at this hour, not so Manhattan's East Side. I was delighted to walk out into a crowded, jostling street, where kids were still playing. I looked into the dimly lit hallways of the tenement houses and remembered that, here, many families shared a bathroom down the hall. Our own little bathroom in Brooklyn was a luxury.

Aunt Becky, rosy-cheeked in her cherry red hat, was waiting under the theater marquee. She gave me a hug and a kiss. "Just in time."

We joined the throngs of excited people milling up the stairs to the balcony. When we were seated, with our coats and hats off, Aunt Becky turned to me. "You know, we'll be meeting John tonight," she said, squeezing my arm.

I nodded happily. Before we could say anything else, the lady on the other side began to speak to me.

"For Jenny Goldstein, I always need two handkerchiefs," she said, digging into a large bag.

I had hoped we'd be seeing a musical like *The Mikado* so I could pick up some pointers. But this was going to be a drama.

The lights dimmed and I gave all my attention to the stage. When the curtain rose, there was a stir of recognition from the audience. They were looking at a perfect likeness of a *shtetl*, a small town like one most of the audience had left behind in Europe when they came to America.

The Yiddish being spoken on the stage was a little hard for me to follow, but I soon understood that the heroine was leaving her home to join her sweetheart in America. It was a sad scene when she left her parents. It was clear that many in the audience had experienced a similar farewell, and I could hear many sniffles and sighs.

When the curtain went down on the first act, there were red-eyed people all around us. Bags of food were being opened, and the smells of salami, roasted chicken, and other delicious food wafted past my nose. I was sorry I'd been too excited to eat my supper, because I was hungry now.

I looked down into the orchestra. "Aunt Becky, it seems that people down there don't get as hungry as people up here."

She laughed. "After the show, we're meeting John at the Second Avenue Delicatessen."

"Great. I'm starved."

The woman next to me evidently was listening. "If you're hungry, here, eat." She took out of her bag a thick slice of rye bread that had a garlic-rubbed crust and was smeared with chicken fat. Whenever Mama rendered the fat from the chicken, she gave us this for a treat. My mouth watered for the woman's bread, but I hesitated.

Aunt Becky said, "That's very nice of you. My niece is hungry."

So, during the second act, I sat back and munched on the delicious bread. On stage, Friedele discovered she was no longer wanted by the man for whom she had traveled across the ocean. Proudly, she refused to take any money from him and was left penniless and sick at heart. The poor woman became ill and lingered at death's door.

As each misfortune befell Friedele, I could hear sniffling and crying and blowing of noses. Soon I was wiping my own eyes, and when the lady next to me erupted with "*Oy gevalt,*" I could not hold back my own quivering sigh.

In the third act, the heroine got better, but she wasn't sure life was worth living. Then she met a young man and fell in love with him, and he with her. When the curtain finally came down, everyone in the theater was happy for Friedele.

"I told you with Jenny Goldstein you need more than one handkerchief," my neighbor said, as we stood to leave.

Out in the cold, we walked quickly toward the restaurant and John O'Neill. Aunt Becky looked radiant. I worried about my shabby winter coat and what he would think of me.

"John has heard so much about you that he can't wait to meet you."

"How long have you known him?"

"John was my English teacher three years ago."

"And you've been seeing him since then?"

"No, it began a year later, when I met him in the library."

In front of the brightly lit delicatessen stood a tall, good-looking man, with gray hair at the temples. He came forward in long strides.

"Hello, Becky."

They stood together, her hand in his, just looking at each other. The next moment both turned to me. Now it was my hand being held so warmly by this handsome man with the kindest blue eyes.

"This young lady can't be the little girl you've been talking about so much."

Becky laughed. "You know how girls can grow at this age."

"And pretty too. Now I'll be escorting two beautiful women for the evening."

He tucked each of our arms under his, and we walked into the busy restaurant. While we were enjoying our corned beef sandwiches, John told us stories about his students, each one funnier than the one before.

Then he turned to me and said in a serious tone, "I understand you are interested in taking voice lessons."

"Yes, very much."

"I have a friend who works in the Bronx Settlement House and runs the music program. I'll talk to him about you."

Then we discussed *The Mikado*, and John had an amusing story about how the composers, Gilbert and Sullivan, could not get along and seldom spoke to each other.

Aunt Becky told us about the poetry course she was taking this term.

"Of course, you are studying Browning," John said. And then he recited "How Do I Love Thee" in such a low, beautiful voice that even I couldn't help but see the passion and love in this man.

I looked at Aunt Becky, so alive, so enrapt, and I knew something then. I was old enough to understand that this was love between a man and a woman. But knowing this sent a chill of fear through me. What was to become of my Aunt Becky?

7

A STIR OF EXCITEMENT went through the Glee Club at Miss Beck's announcement. A week from Monday, she and Mr. Davis would decide who should be given the principal roles in *The Mikado*. "All of you who are interested are invited to try out."

By lucky coincidence a letter from Aunt Becky had arrived that week. Her friend John had arranged for me to see a Mr. Desser at the Bronx Settlement House. I needed Mama's permission.

But Mama was upset about Elliot. Despite boxing lessons, Elliot was still coming home bloodied.

"Did you fight back?" David wanted to know.

"I tried, but he's so big."

"It's no use," Mama said. "We have to see the principal."

"Don't go yet," Michael said. "I have an idea."

"What kind of idea?" I asked.

"That's between Elliot and me. No one's supposed to know what we are planning," he said, sounding important.

I shrugged my shoulders. "What can we lose, Mama?"

"More bloody shirts to wash," she said.

"Anyhow, Mama, this Saturday I want to go to the Bronx Settlement House to see a Mr. Desser, a voice teacher."

"You can't take piano lessons again? It's in the house, and how can a young girl travel by herself to the Bronx? Not by yourself — somebody has to go with you."

"Mama, it's only the Bronx, not Europe." I was up against

a stone wall. "Who can I get? Papa works until noon. Davy practices with his band. I am positively not taking either Elliot or Michael."

Mama shook her head and walked away. David, doing his homework on the dining room table, was my only hope.

"Davy, could you go with me to the Settlement House in the Bronx this Saturday? Mama won't allow me to go alone."

"You mean this Saturday and every Saturday after? You know that's when my band..."

"I know you meet with your band. It would only be for the first time. Anyhow, I don't even know if Mr. Desser will accept me. And next Monday, there's going to be a tryout for *The Mikado*, and I thought..."

"Hey, hold it. You don't think that you can have one easy lesson and you'll be sure to get that part?" He ran his fingers through his hair.

"David!" I shook my head in anger. "Can't you understand the confidence it would give me if I was accepted by a voice teacher?"

"How much will it cost?"

I shook my head. I hadn't the faintest idea.

"Let's not worry about that yet. We'll see what he says when we get there," David said.

"Oh, Davy, thanks." We weren't a hugging family or I would have hugged him. I wanted to take back all the nasty, jealous thoughts I'd ever had of my big brother.

When I went to tell Mama, she had her head in the closet, looking for the special caps the boys wore in the spring.

"Here they are." She held out identical hats for the boys.

"Debbie, the only thing you have to do is get me out of my last class ten minutes early," Michael ordered. "Can you do it?"

"Yes, sir," I couldn't help saying.

Jenny Sharp was absent the next day, so it seemed easy to tell Ben about the twins and why I had to leave early.

"The boys sound like fun," he said with his warm, crinkly smile.

"I never thought of kid brothers as fun. Are yours fun?"

"I don't have any. I am the one and only in my family."

That explained a lot, I thought. I was elated at the ease of our conversation. I didn't mention Mr. Desser, just in case it turned out badly.

There was no trouble getting Michael out of his class. "Now what are you going to do?" I asked him as we walked out of the building.

"Leave it to me. Just wait in the yard."

So that's where I was when, one minute before three, Elliot's class exploded out of the door. The boys and girls swooped down the stairs and ran through the yard to the exits.

Where was Elliot? I must have missed him since he was wearing a spring cap instead of his winter hat. Halfway down the block, I thought I recognized the cap. Elliot looked awfully small, especially since an oversized, chunky kid was chasing him. I decided to catch up with him in case I could help. The bigger boy was gaining on my brother, and I ran faster.

Where was Michael with his big schemes? I was close enough to hear the bully chanting, "Fraidy, fraidy cat." His arms were outstretched to pounce on Elliot, who was a head shorter and only an arm's distance away.

And then, Elliot suddenly spun around. Surprised, the big boy almost ran into him. In the next second I knew it was Michael and not Elliot, but the bully was confused. Michael assumed a fighting position, his fists up and ready. Before the boy could recover his balance, Michael had landed a punch that left the bully on his back, with his hat in the mud. Michael stooped to pick up the filthy hat, and, with all his might, he pushed it into the astonished face. Then he turned and walked away without a word.

At supper, there was nothing but praise for Michael.

Papa joked, "I should have called you David, since you can fight the modern Goliaths."

"How did you change places without anyone seeing you, Michael?" Davy wanted to know.

"Elliot was at the end of the line, and I changed places with him outside in the hallway."

"And we won't have to see Mr. Davis," Mama said, looking happy.

Sometimes it was good to have brothers. I was sure glad to have my big one on Saturday when we both got up early to go to the Settlement House. I enjoyed walking next to this broad-shouldered boy with the wavy hair who was my brother David.

That day I made a new discovery about David. He was funny. All the way to the Bronx, he told me stories that made me laugh. When we reached the old private house with the sign "Bronx Settlement House," I was in a relaxed mood. I left David reading a magazine while I found my way down a corridor with many rooms. From behind the doors, I could hear all kinds of musical sounds.

In front of me was a door with a sign: "Mr. Desser, Director." The word "director" hit me, and suddenly there were butterflies in my stomach. Even as I told myself the worst thing that could happen was that I would be turned down, my legs turned to jelly. If it wouldn't have been so embarrassing, I was ready to find David and go home. I knocked timidly on the door.

"Come in, come in," a German-sounding voice boomed out.

A heavyset man with thinning hair was seated at the piano.

"So, you are Debbie Gold. And you have a voice?"

I nodded. "I think so."

"*Gut. Gut.* So we will hear you sing. What would you like to do for me?"

I gulped, too petrified to remember anything.

"*Ach, Dumkopf* I am." He tapped his head. "You are nervous, of course. Here, sit down, child. Forgive a tired, old man. Tell me about yourself."

So we sat and I told him about my family and about *The Mikado*. He nodded his head, especially when I mentioned Aunt Becky. "My friend John told me about her."

Then Mr. Desser played some simple melodies and I sang them. "Do you know this one?" he asked several times, and I was able to do some of them. He seemed pleased. "You have a good natural voice. But now, I am going to play something you have not heard. Just listen and, if you can, sing it back to me."

It must have been all right because he was smiling. "You have a rare thing — an almost perfect ear."

"Does that mean you will give me lessons?"

"Yes, little lady. You know it means a lot of hard work."

"Mr. Desser, I'll do my best. And, Mr. Desser, how much will it cost?"

I was happy it was the same amount Mama had paid the piano teacher. But I still wanted to talk about *The Mikado*. When I explained there would be tryouts for the lead roles next week, and how anxious I was to do Yum-Yum, he looked at me.

"There's no time today to go through the music with you. But you should have no trouble singing Yum-Yum. You do have one big advantage."

"What's that, Mr. Desser?"

"Well," he scratched his head. "I think you must look like Yum-Yum."

In the train going home, I felt as if I had wings and was flying home. I was ready to face *The Mikado*. I could be Yum-Yum.

8

DESPITE MY new confidence, I knew Jenny Sharp would be very much in the running for the part of Yum-Yum. I had stopped at the library after school on Friday and looked up some books about Japan. One had a picture of a Japanese lady wearing a beautiful kimono, with neat coils of black hair piled on top of her head and ornaments tucked in her hair.

After my meeting with Mr. Desser on Saturday, I went through the closet at home and found a shabby old silk robe that looked like a kimono. I cut it down so only the top was left. I sewed the opening in front and attached two tie strings. Not a bad blouse, I thought, when I tried it on, admiring the effect of the wide sleeves.

With hairpins, I tried rolling my hair into neat coils like the ladies in the pictures. I couldn't get it right at first, but after I rubbed a bit of Vaseline into my hair and borrowed two of Mama's knitting needles for ornaments, I stepped back from the mirror. Now I did look a bit like a Japanese girl. I hoped it was enough to make a difference.

Everyone interested in the tryouts stayed after Glee Club. At three o'clock sharp, Mr. Davis appeared with a long pad of paper and seated himself in the front row, and Miss Beck began.

Each of us was allowed to choose a song to sing when we were called. Four girls before me, including Jenny Sharp, had already requested "The Moon and I," which was also my choice. Jenny was far superior to the other three. When my name was called, I had already tucked up my hair and patted it down with Vaseline. I put the knitting needles into the back roll and walked slowly onto the stage. It was my second try on the stage, but my knees still shook.

When Miss Beck introduced me, I looked at Mr. Davis. I thought I glimpsed a faint smile, and so I missed the cue in the song.

Miss Beck called out my name again. This time, I kept my eyes on the back of the auditorium as we'd been told, and I launched into "The sun whose rays are all ablaze." My voice, shaky at first, steadied as I progressed toward the finish. Now I was almost sure that Mr. Davis had smiled at me.

At last the tryouts were over. A few minutes after Miss Beck and Mr. Davis put their heads together, Miss Beck announced: "The part of Nanki-Poo — Ben Stein. The part of Yum-Yum — Deborah Gold...."

I couldn't hear the rest in the noisy confusion as everyone rushed over to congratulate us. Even Jenny came over, but in a low voice she said to me, "That Japanese get-up was a trick." I ignored her because Ben was shaking my hand and saying how great it would be to play Nanki-Poo to my Yum-Yum.

I couldn't wait to get home and tell my family the good news. I was so anxious to share the big happening that I didn't even ask why Papa was sitting at the kitchen table at this hour. He was thrilled at my success, but not Mama. Mama was gloomy.

"Didn't you hear? I got the main lead. Don't you care, Mama?"

Mama shook her head, as if to clear a mist. "Yes, yes, Debbie, it's good. But Papa — Papa is on strike!"

"Strike!"

I shuddered, remembering the last strike. There was no money for food, and Uncle Pincus was shouting all the time because we had to ask him to lend us money. Worst of all was the constant fear that the strikers would be beaten.

After this bad news, my good news didn't feel so wonderful. Now everyone was worried about money. David was happy for me, but he was more concerned about his earnings. The next day, he told us the milkman could use him to help collect what was owed, as well as to deliver milk. This meant more money for him.

Even the twins had an idea. "We're going to shine shoes after school."

Papa looked worried. "A good idea, but not if you don't get your homework done."

"Don't worry about that, we promise you we'll do our work. But we need help with the shoe boxes."

So David put together two shoe boxes, and Papa advanced them enough money to buy polish, brushes, and cloths. By the end of the week, they had earned enough to pay back the loan.

"Now we work for profit," Michael said happily.

Each night they gave Mama their money. Strangely, they did their homework without any fuss after supper. Was shining shoes such fun?

"Are girls allowed to shine shoes?"

"We never saw a girl doing that."

"Doesn't mean they couldn't." I was getting desperate for money. Baby-watching jobs had dried up. The worst of it was that I had money stashed under my mattress in my store-bought coat fund — nine, no, eight dollars.

The twins knew about the fund, and every night when they gave their money to Mama they taunted me about being a miser. How could I explain how much I needed a new coat, not a miserable hand-me-down? It was a year's savings, and I couldn't stand parting with it.

The next night at the supper table, Mama turned to me. "Tomorrow you will go to see Mr. Pofsky. He has a job for you."

"What could I do in Mr. Pofsky's grocery store?"

"It's not for the store. His son needs somebody to help him."

"You mean Loony Eddie?" Michael asked. "He's got a big head, and spit comes out of his mouth all the time."

"But, Mama, you should have asked me about the job first. Don't forget, I have to be at rehearsals twice a week."

"So tell it to Mr. Pofsky. A job is a job, and already we owe Mr. Pofsky money."

I rushed home after school to change my dress and had to listen to Michael warning me not to sit too close to Loony Eddie.

Many times I'd been to Mr. Pofsky's grocery, but today it was different and I hesitated at the door. Inside was the familiar smell of dry cereals, mingled with freshly ground coffee and soured milk.

Mr. Pofsky, a broad man in his heavy sweater and white apron, was busy with some customers and didn't look up. I waited at the counter and watched the grocer's pale face as he hacked out a lump of butter from the tub.

When he saw me, he motioned with his head for me to go to the back of the store, where his family lived. "They're waiting for you," he said in his polite voice.

I ducked through the heavy drapes hung in the doorway and found myself in a large combination living room and kitchen. The ceiling was high and waffled, and dull, drab linoleum covered the floor. The furniture was sparse: a coffee-colored porcelain table surrounded by four dark wooden chairs. In the opposite corner was a brown leather couch.

Mrs. Pofsky, in a bright-red apron, was cooking a savory stew. "Debbie, come in. We're waiting for you." We turned to Eddie, who was sitting on the couch, neatly dressed in tan knickers and a sweater.

"Debbie is going to read to you, Eddie," his mother said. Eddie's small, blue eyes lit up with joy and his big head rolled to one side. When he drooled, Mrs. Pofsky took the clean, folded handkerchief from Eddie's pocket and dabbed his mouth dry.

"I didn't bring anything to read to him, Mrs. Pofsky."

"How about the Sunday comics? Eddie loves them." Eddie clapped his hands and gurgled a happy sound.

"First, why don't you pick some cookies for both of you?"

Back in the store, I walked around the cookie tins and carefully lifted the glass covers until the bag was filled with fig newtons, gingersnaps, sugar wafers, and molasses cookies with white icing.

I returned with the goodies and sat on the couch a small distance away from Eddie. He pored over the pictures with me and roared with laughter at the Katzenjammer Kids. Before I realized it, we were sitting very close, and when he drooled, I reached for his handkerchief and patted his mouth dry.

The hour went by quickly, and it was clear that Eddie had understood everything I had read to him. My goodbye and "I'll be back" was greeted with much head rolling and joyful noises.

I walked home, savoring the good feeling I had because Eddie had so enjoyed what I did for him. Best of all, I had decided to give Papa my coat money to help pay the rent that was due.

9

IT SEEMED that Esther and I had been talking about first dates forever. We were almost fourteen and it still hadn't happened. But after rehearsals for *The Mikado* got under way, I had a feeling it wouldn't be long.

It had become easier to talk to Ben, although our conversations were usually as Nanki-Poo and Yum-Yum, or about something in the play. But I didn't blush as much and could always think of something to say.

The only embarrassment occurred on stage when Nanki-Poo was supposed to kiss his beloved during a duet. We stood so close that I could see the down on Ben's upper lip. After his first attempt, Miss Beck suggested that he only pretend to kiss me. I must admit I was relieved.

The cast kidded us about the kissing, especially Iz Berg.

"May I walk with the two greatest lovers on stage?" he asked, as he joined Ben and me on our way to the ice cream parlor after rehearsal.

"We would be honored to have the Mikado's favorite hatchet man walk with us," was Ben's reply. Iz played the role of Ko-Ko, the Lord High Executioner, and he was just as funny offstage as he was on. Lanky, with freckles and sandy brown hair, he was not exactly the Rudolph Valentino type. I couldn't help comparing him with Ben, who looked great in a tan sweater, tweed knickers, and a bow tie that showed off his handsome profile and his dark, slicked-down hair.

We pushed two tables together at the ice cream parlor and all sat down. Jenny, who was given the role of Katisha in the play, was on one side of Ben. What did I care? Today I was feeling on top of the world because Miss Beck had complimented me on my performance.

We all went Dutch treat, and I had just enough for a cone, even though everyone was ordering frappes and sundaes. I was relieved to hear Iz order a cone first.

"Is anyone interested in going to see *The Mikado* done by professionals at the Wintergarden on Broadway?" Ben asked. "My folks offered to pick up tickets for anyone who'd like to go."

Everyone's hand shot up, except mine.

"It's unanimous then."

"Debbie's not going," Jenny announced. Every eye was on me.

"I have to check with my mother," I said, somewhat lamely. How could I ask for money for the theater when Papa was still striking?

Later, when we were putting on our coats, Ben leaned over and said in a low voice, "Of course, I'd like you to come as my date."

"I'll have to get my mother's permission," I said. Couldn't he hear how loud my heart was beating? He reached over, squeezed my hand, and winked at me.

It was so exciting to think about my first date — and with Ben Stein! — that I hardly realized Iz was walking beside me over the bridge.

"I guess you didn't know that I'm from your part of town?" Iz said.

I shook my head.

"Well, if you ever took your eyes off Ben Stein, you might have noticed me around," he said with a smile.

It turned out that Iz passed my house every day as he walked to and from school. By the time I got to my door, I knew that Iz lived with his widowed mother and two younger sisters. After he checked on the younger children, he would be off to his job at the druggist's, delivering medicines.

"It must be hard without your father."

He nodded, looking sad for the first time. He was always such a clown. "It's going to make it harder to become a doctor."

"A doctor! That takes a lot of money."

"It does. But as soon as I have my working papers, I'll get a real job after school for some real money."

I was so engrossed in what Iz was saying that I'd almost forgotten about Ben asking me out. But now I bounded up the stairs, eager to tell Mama and discuss what to wear on my first date.

When Mama suggested that the blue serge dress she had made for me would be nice, I had to disagree. How could I explain that homemade dresses were not the thing for dates? I needed to buy a ready-made blouse to go with a brown skirt that wasn't too bad. It was the coat that plagued me. What could be done with this gray horror?

"Why don't you get a bright woolen scarf?" Esther suggested, when I stopped by her apartment to tell her my news. "If mine weren't so shabby, I'd loan it to you."

"If only I hadn't given my father all my money."

There was one glimmer of hope — Mr. Pofsky. He had promised to pay me at the end of the month. "We'll settle all money matters then," he had said.

It wouldn't be much, but I had an idea. Mrs. Pofsky frequently had headaches and couldn't work in the store. When I got there and found her with a wet rag over her eyes, I spoke up.

"Would you like me to help, Mrs. Pofsky?"

"If only you could, I would rest my head."

Eddie was expecting me to read to him. "Eddie," I whispered, "Could you finish looking at the pictures yourself? I'm going to help your father."

He drooled and looked unhappy. I wiped his mouth and tucked the white handkerchief back into his pocket. Then I walked through the curtain and went up to Mr. Pofsky. There were a lot of customers waiting.

"Would you like some help, Mr. Pofsky?"

Mr. Pofsky turned and peered over his glasses. "Could you, Debbie?" He looked doubtful.

"I'll try." I put on Mrs. Pofsky's apron and faced the four ladies and a boy whose head barely reached above the counter.

"Who is next?" I asked timidly.

The boy's order was drowned out by a lady with a big voice. "Me," she said, "and I want a can of salmon."

I reached for it and placed it on the counter. "What else?"

"Pound of coffee, mixed."

There were four sacks of coffee beans. I took some from each until the paper bag felt like a pound. It was a little over so I made the correction, then poured all of it into the coffee grinder.

It was a short order and I totaled the prices that Mr. Pofsky gave me on the outside of the bag. After I gave the lady her correct change from the cash box, I called out, "Next."

Again the little boy tried to say something, but the buxom woman next to him spoke louder.

"I think the boy is next," I said, and got an angry look from the woman.

The boy, who wanted a pint of milk, handed a metal quart pail over the counter. I turned to the big vat of milk that stood in a wooden tub surrounded by ice. It had a wooden cover with a trap door in the middle.

"How does it open?" I whispered to Mr. Pofsky.

"Open the little door." When I did I could see two long-handled measures. I grasped one and then the other, and decided the lighter one must be the pint. When I poured its contents into the quart pail, it came halfway.

"What else?" I clamped the cover on the pail and handed it to the boy. That was all he wanted, so I dropped the money into the cash box.

"You're doing good," Mr. Pofsky said.

"So how long do I have to wait?" It was the buxom woman.

"What can I get you?"

"A quarter pound of butter." I hesitated and wished Mr. Pofsky could do this one. I started to suggest she wait, but she looked so angry I lost my nerve. The tub of butter was inside the glass door of the icebox. It looked so easy when Mr. Pofsky did it.

I pulled out the knife stuck in the tub of butter and carefully carved out a chunk. I dropped it on the waiting paper and put it on the scale. My face turned beet red — it weighed three-quarters of a pound.

Mr. Pofsky came over and instructed, "A quarter of a pound is one inch wide and two inches long. Try it, Debbie."

Incredibly, when I judged these dimensions, the butter weighed the exact amount. I removed it from the scale.

"Just a minute. I want to see the weight," the customer said. I returned it to the scale.

"It's short," she crowed.

I was just about to point out that it was exactly on the quarter mark when Mr. Pofsky came over to say, "That's right, Mrs. Herman." He winked at me. "Put another little pat on." The woman smiled as she left.

The hour went by quickly, and I could see that Mr. Pofsky was pleased with me.

"Could you use me again?" I asked him.

Mr. Pofsky scratched his head. "Sure, I could. Mrs. Pofsky would like that. But Eddie, he loves you to read to him."

"I'll try to do both. When it isn't busy in the store, I'll read to Eddie."

So I did and it worked out pretty well. Payday was next week, and I couldn't wait to find out how much I had earned. Whatever it was, it was going to be spent for some part of an outfit for my first date.

On payday, when Mr. Pofsky asked me to sit down so we could square accounts, I was more than ready.

"First, Debbie, I want you to know that you have made Eddie happy. And now, since you're helping in the store, we are all happy about you. At first we thought we'd pay you fifteen cents an hour, but since we are so pleased, we decided, my wife and I, that you are worth twenty cents an hour. How's that?" Mr. Pofsky was beaming.

"Thank you." I was trying to figure how many hours I'd worked for the last few weeks and multiply it by twenty cents. I didn't really notice when Mr. Pofsky pulled down his black "owing book." But I focused in when he thumbed to the page marked "Gold" and wetted the stub of the pencil in his mouth.

"Let's see..." He wrote the sum down and seemed to be subtracting. "That's better." He must have caught my surprised look. "Didn't your mother explain the arrangement?" I shook my head.

"You're not fourteen yet, and your mother owes me a lot of money and..."

"I understand."

"I can't tell you, Debbie, how lucky your mother is to have a daughter like you. My wife and I would thank God every day for a child like you."

After that I could do nothing but say good night and go home — without a penny, without a way to get what I so desperately needed for my first date and my first Broadway show.

10

I COULDN'T HIDE my disappointment. Mama took one look at me and knew what had happened, but she said nothing. Everybody handed Mama all the money they earned, and so my contribution came in groceries. She may have been right, but I was angry.

When Michael asked how much Mr. Pofsky had paid me I said, "Nothing."

"Nothing?"

Mama explained.

"That is a funny way to get paid," Papa said. "I would like to give you a dollar for your new blouse. I wish it could be more."

"If it's all right with Mama, I'll give you a dollar, too," Davy said. Mama nodded.

"We'll chip in twenty-five cents each," Michael and Elliot said.

I scraped together some loose change and added up two dollars and seventy-four cents. Would it be enough to buy a blouse and a scarf? If so, I'd love my family forever.

I hurried to the pushcarts, determined to find what I needed. I pushed my way through the crowds until I found the blouse store. There were some beautiful ones, but they were too expensive.

"Haven't you anything for less money?" I asked the lady.

She looked through the rack of blouses. "Here's one. It's only two dollars and forty-nine cents."

She held up a satiny-looking blouse with a row of cute bows that started at the collar and went down to the waist. Were there too many bows? I tried it on and it fit perfectly. The bows were just right, and the deep-pink color was good with my complexion.

"I would take it if it were one dollar and fifty cents."

"I'll ask the owner."

I kept my fingers crossed. When she said it was okay, I was elated. Now for the scarf.

I headed for the pushcart down the block, where scarves were piled helter-skelter. I studied each one carefully until I found the softest gold-and-orange plaid. I tried it over my coat and it was perfect. A good part of the coat was covered, and I knew I just had to have it.

I looked at the peddler, but couldn't see his face. From his woolen helmet, only his eyes and mouth were visible. He wore an old army coat and had wrapped strips of khaki cloth around his legs for warmth. He looked a little bit frightening.

"How...how much is this please?" I asked.

His mouth opened. "Two dollars and ninety-eight cents."

My heart sank. How did Mama do her bargaining? Usually she would cut the price in half and start to bargain from there. But I couldn't do that since I had to finish with a dollar and a quarter.

"I'll give you one dollar for it." My voice was a whisper.

The discolored teeth in his mouth spat out, "Girlie, you must be crazy. I'm in business to make a living."

I swallowed hard. "How about one dollar and fifteen cents?"

"Why don't you pick a cheaper scarf instead of my best one?" He was screaming. "The cheapest is two dollars."

"Mister, would you take one dollar and a quarter, please?"

"A dollar fifty cents, take it or leave it."

"But I only have one dollar and a quarter. Mister, I really must have that scarf."

He looked at me and said nothing. His black eyes glowered

at me. Then he threw up his hands and shook his head. "All right! All right! Money you can't always make."

He put the scarf in a bag and I handed him the money. "A penny is missing," he announced.

"I know, and I'm sorry. That's all the money I have."

"Customers like you I don't need. Go, already."

"Thank you. Thank you very much." I was glad to get away from him.

I hugged my packages, eager to get home to share my bargains with my family. Today I understood why Mama always said blood is thicker than water. I was grateful to all my family.

I had told Mr. Desser I was going to see *The Mikado* on Saturday and wouldn't be in for my lesson. By Saturday, my skirt had been cleaned and pressed; my hair was waved and shiny clean; my nails were polished. And I couldn't wait for eleven o'clock, when Ben would pick me up. Papa and my brothers all agreed I looked very nice in the store-bought blouse. Only Mama was a bit reserved in her praise.

I was uneasy about Ben coming to my home, but there was no choice. For a date, the boy must pick you up. At least it was Saturday, when the house looked as good as it could, after its weekly cleaning on Thursday and Friday. Everybody was at home; even the twins refused to play outside.

When the knock sounded I tried not to run to the door. It was Ben, cap in hand, and looking very handsome.

"Come in, Ben. Meet my family."

I introduced him to Mama, who nodded her greeting. Papa shook hands with him, and so did David.

"And this is Michael and Elliot."

"Hello," Ben said. "I know all about you two."

"Yeah?" Michael was not impressed. "Are you Debbie's fellah?"

"Ben," I interrupted. "Look at the clock. We ought to get going."

He helped me on with my coat, and I was really glad for

my new scarf. I threw it around the collar and smoothed it down the front of my coat. Even Mama's eyes lit up with approval.

I was glad to escape from my family, but it seemed all the neighbors were out on the street, greeting me and glancing at Ben out of the corners of their eyes.

Finally, we were on the bridge and really alone. Ben had not said much. Was he thinking about our crowded flat or that my family looked like greenhorns? I needed to say something, but what? And then it came to me.

"I can't wait to see *The Mikado* performed on Broadway."

"Me, too."

After that, the conversation was easy. Everybody was waiting for us at the school, and Ben introduced his parents. On the train, I found myself next to Mr. Stein, a handsome, gray-haired man, an older version of Ben. He told me that, although he was born in Russia, Mrs. Stein was an American-born woman. At the other end of the train, Jenny was having a conversation with Mrs. Stein, who was wearing a brown fur coat and an elegant hat.

Then Mr. Stein confided that he hoped his son would become a lawyer — something Mr. Stein had always wanted to be.

"He'll probably be a good one," I said. Mr. Stein looked pleased.

At the theater, Ben's seat was next to mine. The Wintergarden Theatre was more elegant than the Yiddish one on Second Avenue. But the magic moment was the same in both places. I held my breath for the few seconds before the curtain went up.

And there it was — the make-believe Japanese land of Titipu, with richly dressed nobles strolling around. Then Nanki-Poo entered, a guitar on his back and a bundle of ballads in his hands.

We were a most attentive group. Each of us looked for our counterpart on the stage. I was enthralled with Yum-Yum, who looked so petite, especially next to the big Katisha. It was a marvel of acting and singing, and there was much laughter from the audience.

Watching this actress, I made a mental note to remember to take very small steps when I played Yum-Yum, and to bow often. The fan that Yum-Yum carried would be a nice prop if I could find one.

When the lights went on, we all sat back and smiled at each other, too thrilled and excited to comment on what we'd seen. It wasn't until we were in the ice cream parlor, with its dark mahogany paneling, that the torrent of conversation erupted.

"Did you see…?"

"Did you notice…?"

"I'm going to…"

"Wasn't it…?"

Mr. and Mrs. Stein, our hosts, must have been grateful when we all dug into the delicious ice cream and there was something like quiet.

Mrs. Stein was sitting next to me, and in between spoonfuls of ice cream we spoke. Her English was perfect — a rare treat for me since most of the mothers I knew could hardly utter one complete sentence in English. With her fur coat off, I could see she was wearing a nice suit and a lovely, shell-pink blouse with the merest touch of lace. It made my blouse look too much — too shiny, too cute, with too many bows. Oh, well, it wasn't enough to ruin my day.

"Ben tells us you are taking voice lessons," Mrs. Stein said, and I told her about the Bronx Settlement House and Mr. Desser.

"I am really looking forward to seeing your Yum-Yum," was the last thing she said to me.

It wasn't until Ben was walking me home that I realized he and I hadn't been alone most of the day.

"I had a great time, Ben," I said as we neared my house. Dusk was just beginning to settle in the streets.

"Hey, me too." We talked more about how the actors we'd

seen today performed their roles as we slowly walked up the stairs.

"Thanks for inviting me," I said when we reached the landing, and Ben turned to me. His face was coming toward mine and I knew I was going to be kissed. Somehow I didn't get my face into the right position, and the kiss landed between my nose and my cheek. Before I could make the correction, Ben had bounded down the stairs.

All in all, it was a good first date, I wrote in my diary. The best part was all the hints I had learned from the professional Yum-Yum on the stage. I was anxious to try them.

11

WITH ONE WEEK to go until opening night of *The Mikado*, the cast was at a high pitch. The Pofskys had been told not to expect me at the store next week. Anyhow, the strike at Papa's company had been settled, so he was working and money problems weren't so pressing. I was giving Yum-Yum my all.

I tried to remember everything about the way Yum-Yum had been performed at the Wintergarden. If only I could stand in the wings and watch how the actress walked, how she stood, what she did with her hands, but that wasn't possible.

Then an unexpected thing happened. On Thursday, Miss Lee returned our Patrick Henry report to Mary Regan and me with a request that it be rewritten by Monday. She planned to enter it in a citywide contest for papers on famous Americans.

"Where shall we work?" Mary asked.

I knew I couldn't offer my home. "How about the library?"

Mary shook her head. "Miss Williams wouldn't allow us to talk." I nodded. "How about coming to my place?" said Mary. "Then you could see my father's library."

"Great!"

"And Debbie, I just remembered my Aunt Irene is coming for dinner on Friday. You know, she's the one I told you about."

"You mean the aunt who performed Yum-Yum profession-ally?"

"That's the one. Would you like to come for dinner?"

I hesitated. "I'd have to ask my mother."

"And tell her we always have fish on Friday night."

"I will. I'll let you know tomorrow."

"You know, maybe you ought to sleep over Friday night — we'd have a whole day Saturday to work on the report."

This was really unexpected. "You mean I'd sleep at your house Friday night?"

"Sure."

"I'll let you know tomorrow what my mother says."

What a break! But when I should have been running home to ask Mama, my feet felt like lead. I just knew Mama was going to be six feet tall, and I almost didn't have the energy to tackle her. My stomach felt queasy.

Mama was standing at the sink peeling potatoes, and I didn't waste any time.

"Hello, Mama. Listen, Mama, Mary Regan invited me to sleep over at her house tomorrow night. I'm going to meet her Aunt Irene who used to be a singer and who's going to give me hints. And we have to write the Patrick Henry re-port over again and I thought..."

Mama turned slowly, a puzzled look on her face. "What are you saying, Debbie? You want to sleep at a Mary Regan's house? And you're going to eat there, too?"

"Yes, yes. They eat fish on Friday night. Mama, you can't understand how important this is for me."

"It's *meshugge* for a Jewish girl to eat and sleep in a Mary Regan's house."

"There's nothing crazy about it. Please listen. I'll explain it again." I tried to tone down the shriek in my voice. Mama looked taller than six feet already and I was getting desper-ate.

"And what about the singing lessons you had to have? Two Saturdays a month you go to the Bronx for lessons.

Last Saturday all we heard about is that play. This Saturday, too, you have other plans."

I tried again to explain about the Patrick Henry paper, but when I finished, Mama shook her head in disapproval. I ran out, slamming the kitchen door hard, my anger choking me.

Crash!

I didn't open the door until the terrible sound of falling, splintering glass had stopped. Mama, pale and thin-lipped, was standing stock still in the middle of the disaster of broken glass strewn all over the kitchen floor.

It was the beautiful set of pitcher and glasses that had stood so proudly on the icebox. Mama had saved a long time to buy it, and now my temper had broken it.

"I'm sorry, Mama."

"Sorry! Does sorry bring back my set?"

Mama wouldn't let me help her clean it up. I went to my room and threw myself on the bed and cried. Everything suddenly seemed too much. So many things had been going my way, and now it all seemed a mess. I didn't want to see David when he came in later and stood by my bed.

"Mama told me what happened." His voice accused me.

I dug my head deeper into the pillow.

"You can't blame Mama for the way she feels," he said.

"What do you mean?" I turned my head away from the pillow. "Mama is old-fashioned and doesn't know anything. How can you side with her?"

"Don't you remember the terrible thing that happened to her when she was a young girl in Europe?"

Of course, I remembered. How could anyone forget such a horrible story? Mama, who grew up in a small town in Russia, was only twelve that day. Her parents had left her at home with the baby, who was sleeping in his crib. Mama had just finished scrubbing the floor when she heard shouting outside. She froze with fear when she looked out the window. A gang of Cossacks were shooting and smashing their way down the street. It was a *pogrom!*

Mama knew their lives were in danger. They would have to go into the hiding place their father had prepared. If the Cossacks came in and saw nobody, perhaps they would go away. The baby was fast asleep and would cry if she woke him and took him into the hiding place. Then they would both be discovered. She made a split-second decision.

She propped pillows around him and piled blankets on top. After making sure he wouldn't suffocate, she crawled behind the bed and down into the dark hole her father had dug for them. She closed the trap door after her and huddled in the darkness.

A minute later, Mama could hear the door being smashed and then the sound of loud, angry voices. There was a horrible banging and shattering as the soldiers trooped through the house destroying china and furniture — including the baby's crib.

The horror of what happened made Mama ill for a long time. She blamed herself for the baby's death. But worse, since then she had never quite trusted anyone who wasn't Jewish.

Yes, I remembered that story. "But Davy," I reminded him, "that was a long time ago and in another country. This is America."

I fell into an exhausted sleep. It was light outside when I woke up. My dress was a wrinkled mess and I was groggy as I staggered out of bed. The boys were eating their oatmeal and Papa was feeding Donny when I walked into the kitchen.

"What time is it, Papa?" I asked, pouring cold water on my face from the kitchen sink.

"Almost time to go to school, Debbie. You slept all afternoon and all night. Are you all right?"

"My stomach hurts. Maybe because I haven't eaten." I buttered a roll and poured coffee into a half cup of hot milk. "Where's Mama?"

"Mrs. Fein's baby is sick." Papa shook his head. "Mama told me what happened yesterday. Debbie, that's a bad temper."

I couldn't help the tear that dropped.

"About Mary Regan," he paused, "I told Mama if it is so important to you, you should have permission to go."

"Oh, Papa." I hugged him. A father is what a girl needs, I decided, as I changed into another dress. I was late, but I didn't feel like running today. Must be some kind of spring fever.

Mary was excited when I told her I could visit her.

"Oh, Debbie, that's great. We'll really do a job on Patrick Henry. How would you like to be picked up at five?"

"Picked up?"

"Sure, we'll drive over. My father is home at that hour."

"I'd appreciate it. For some reason I'm kind of tired today."

There was no rehearsal on Friday, so I would have time to clean up and pack. The day seemed endless before I got to my last class at school. I was putting on my green gym suit in the locker room, as was Jenny.

"I hear you're sleeping over at Mary's," she said.

"That's right."

"I thought Jewish people had to eat certain food." Her voice had a sneer to it.

"I'll just have to be a little careful," I answered, pulling on my socks.

"Hey, that's my sock you're putting on, Debbie," Jenny said.

"Your sock!??" I knew Jenny was not happy that Ben and I were doing nicely. I knew it might hurt her that her friend Mary invited me to sleep over at her house. But a sock is a sock. "How could it be yours?"

"It's simple. Mine are missing. Those socks you're putting on are my size; they're too big for you. And they look just like my missing pair."

It was true they were large, too large for me. But Mama always bought that way. "Sorry, Jenny. I always wear my socks loose. These are definitely mine." I tied my shoelaces and walked out, leaving a fuming Jenny.

She looked daggers at me when Miss Gibbs marked her

down for incomplete dress, but I was too tired to care. I should have asked to be excused, but I was squad leader that week. After we'd gone through our exercises, we broke into squads for competitive games, my group playing dodge-the-ball against Jenny's group.

Usually very agile, I managed to stay in to the last. Today Josephine, the tallest girl in the class, and I were still left; we looked like a Mutt-and-Jeff act. I thought I was doing very well, considering how I felt. In the next moment I spotted the ball poised in Jenny's hand. Before I could move, it was flashing toward me with murderous speed and accuracy. It smashed into my right side and I toppled over.

When I opened my eyes I was looking up from the floor at a circle of frightened girls. Miss Gibbs pushed her way toward me. "Step aside, girls. Give her air. Did she faint? Who did it?"

"I'm sorry, Miss Gibbs." It was Jenny. "I was aiming at Josephine, but Debbie must have stepped into the path."

"I'm all right," I managed to say and stood up, my legs wobbly. The bench felt good for the rest of the period.

At the three o'clock bell, I decided not to mention being hit by the ball to Mama. It might be just the excuse she needed to keep me home. I would say nothing, just wash up, pack, and rest. It wasn't until I opened our apartment door to the usual Friday pandemonium that I knew I was really sick.

12

I MUST HAVE BEEN sick in the head to allow Mary and her father to pick me up that day. I'd actually forgotten what a mountain of cleaning had to be done on Fridays. How could I do everything and be ready on time?

Panic hit me, but with it came a surge of energy. I forgot about the pain in my side. Nothing was going to stop me from staying over with Mary.

Through the bathroom door I could hear Mama giving Donny his bath.

"Mama," I called through the door. "Mr. Regan and Mary are picking me up at five o'clock."

No answer. I opened the door and went quickly into the steamy bathroom. Mama was kneeling beside the tub. Donny, glad to see me, sent up a spray of water with his little hands.

"Mama, did you hear me?"

"I heard."

"I'm going to scrub the floor and try to get the house in order before they come." My voice shook. Mama looked up at me but said nothing.

Michael and Elliot were having their milk and cookies when I went in the kitchen. "Boys, am I glad to see you. Would you hurry up and help me clean the house?"

"The guys are waiting for a stoopball game. We promised them," Michael said, his mouth full of cookies.

"Please!"

"What's the trouble, Debbie?" Elliot asked.

"Mr. Regan and Mary are picking me up at five today."

"We won't play long," Michael promised. "We'll be right back."

Right back after their game, I thought. Not very likely. Should I do the boys' polishing first or my own work?

"Mama!" I screamed through the closed bathroom door.

Mama stepped out. "What's the matter?"

I told her about the twins. She made a disapproving face and stepped back into the bathroom. I decided to do the polishing first and then scrub the floor. Mama came out carrying Donny, damp and dewy clean.

As I was getting the polishing rags out, the door opened and it was Elliot. "I came back to help," he said.

Michael was in back of him, muttering, "That Elliot, he's a pain." I was happy to hand them the rags for their chores.

I hurried to my weekly job of scrubbing the kitchen floor. Down on my knees I dipped the stiff brush into the pail of hot water and rubbed it against the yellow bar of soap. I scrubbed a small area, then wiped up the dirty suds with the hot clean rags. Inch by inch, the blue and green linoleum sprang to life, and the dirt retreated.

I was wringing out the rags to return to the pail for next week's washing when the pain in my side suddenly returned. For a moment I shut my eyes. When I was able to catch my breath again, I wiped the beads of perspiration from my forehead. It was hot in the kitchen.

I still had to get cleaned up and packed. I gave myself a quick sponging, scrubbing my knees, then slipped into my blue serge dress and brushed my hair. The face in the mirror seemed unusually pale.

I had to decide what to pack. The old blue bathrobe was ruled out. Thank goodness, Mama had just sewn me a new pair of soft, pink pajamas. I added my toothbrush and picked out a change of clothing for Saturday morning. Now I needed the valise.

"David, would you mind getting the valise from the shelf in the closet?"

"Kind of big for so few things."

"Just get it down, please." But when he took down the valise, I knew he was right. It was much too big and bulky.

"What am I going to do?"

"How about one of the twins' school bags?"

"Good idea." But when I checked them, they were too shabby.

"So use a paper bag," Mama suggested.

I couldn't stop myself from saying, "Thank you, Mama. I don't want to look as if I just got off the boat." Then I had an idea. "Mama, could I use the little rug you bought for Papa?"

"It's for Papa to put his feet down so he shouldn't feel the cold floor."

"I'm sure Papa wouldn't mind if I borrowed it for one night. We'll run up a loose seam on both sides."

"How are you going to hold it?" Davy asked.

"Could you make handles for it?"

"There's some old broomsticks in my shop. I could cut them up. It might do." Davy went to his "shop" in the corner of the cellar, where he was making a crystal radio set.

Mama had already opened the sewing machine and was threading it. I brought her the small rug and she sewed two hems on it. She was muttering something under her breath about children. I had only fifteen minutes to go. Where was David? Could it take this long to cut two broomsticks? Sometimes he forgot himself and started to work on that crystal set.

"Mama, I'm going down to see what's taking David so long." As I started out, the door opened. It was David with the broomstick handle freshly cut in two pieces.

"Please hurry." Impatiently I grabbed one handle and tried to push it into the top hem, but it stuck. "It's not working," I cried.

"Let me try, Debbie," said my big brother.

"Yes, you're a genius."

"Save the genius label for when I finish the crystal set. Then we'll be receiving music from Manhattan."

"Imagine — all the way from Manhattan" was all that I could say in the face of such talent.

When I placed my belongings into the snug little bag, it was just five o'clock. The house looked as good as it could and Mama was wearing a clean apron. But the twins had on their smudged work shirts. How could I introduce such dirty little boys to Mr. Regan?

"Mama, tell those boys to clean themselves up."

"We were cleaning. What did you expect?" Michael was indignant. I knew I didn't have the strength to battle them.

David came over to me. "Take it easy. Your friend Mary must have some idea how we live. If she's really your friend, it won't matter. If not, then you shouldn't care."

It sounded so right when he said it. But when I glanced out of the window and saw the black car pull up to the curb, I had an idea.

"Would it be all right if I went down to meet Mary and her father? They just pulled up."

"Hey, they've got a Maxwell," Elliot announced from the window.

"Davy, go with your sister." Mama had a hurt look in her eyes that I tried not to see.

Mr. Regan was just coming around the car when we got down to the street. "I saw you from the window. This is my brother David."

Mary introduced her father to us. Tall, with a droop to his shoulders, he peered down at me through his heavy-rimmed glasses and smiled. "Very nice to meet you, Debbie." Then he turned to shake hands with David and they spoke cordially for a few minutes.

At last we were off. It felt good to sink into the upholstered seat and watch the familiar streets disappear into the soft dusk.

13

THE CAR moved past our school and turned south. The uneven apartment houses changed to rows of brownstones, flanked by sycamore trees.

"Here we are," Mary said as we stopped in front of a brownstone with a red door.

Inside, the dark-wooded hallway smelled of lemon oil. It was dimly lit by a cupid lamp, which stood on a pedestal at the foot of a curving stairway. We hung our coats on hooks on either side of a long mirror. I just had a chance to smooth my hair before Mary introduced me to a gray-haired woman, Mrs. O'Rourke.

"Tillie, is Mrs. Regan at home yet?" Mary's father asked.

"No, Mr. Regan, I'm expecting her any minute."

"My mother is at the hospital board meeting or somewhere doing charity work. Lucky for us Tillie's a good cook. Come along, Debbie."

We were entering the largest, airiest, and most beautiful room I'd ever seen. The setting sun glowed through the sheer curtains and fell on a lavender silk shawl draped gracefully over the baby grand piano. It had huge, shiny birds embroidered on it and long, silky fringes. I think it was called a Spanish shawl.

To one side of the fireplace was a wooden carved settee with crocheted doilies on the arms and the back. Vases of fresh flowers seemed to be all over the room. In the corner near a window with red velvet drapes was a potted fern. Big, soft, comfortable armchairs made the room look inviting.

"What a beautiful room," I said as I headed for one of the chairs.

"Let me give you the tour first," Mary said.

When I turned to follow Mary, a pain flashed up my right side and I dropped my bag.

Mary called down from the top of the stairs, "This way, please," in her best tour-guide voice. The pain subsided and I was able to pick up the little carpetbag and slowly climb the stairs.

"On the second floor, for the housing of parents, we also have the library," Mary said.

We were looking at a small room whose walls were lined with books from floor to ceiling. I could only shake my head in disbelief.

"You're welcome to look around and borrow any book, Debbie," Mr. Regan said. "Mary told me how anxious you were to see the library. If you'll step in, I'll show you how the books are arranged."

"Not now, Daddy. I'm going to take Debbie up to her room."

"Anytime at all, Debbie, anytime."

"You'd be gone for hours if I let Daddy get you in the library."

We walked up another flight of stairs. "This is the Junior Department — in other words, where I live, if you can call sleeping and doing homework living."

We giggled and Mary threw open the door to her bedroom. "Enter my domain."

Here before my eyes was my dream room. The tiniest rosebuds trailed on the wallpaper, framing white, starched curtains that crisscrossed the windows. A gleaming brass bed stood in the middle of the pinkest of rugs. On a shelf near the bed sat a collection of Kewpie dolls, all fat-cheeked and wide-eyed with their hair done up in topknots. And right above the bed hung a large, gold crucifix. I had never been so close to one, and my eyes riveted on the drooping figure on the cross.

Mary, noticing my intense stare, explained, "My god-mother gave it to me when I was born." I couldn't take my eyes off the cross. "Haven't you ever seen one before?" Mary asked.

"Of course, but never this close." I was embarrassed. "I didn't realize they were hung in homes."

Mary laughed. "I guess you don't have many Catholic friends. Anyhow, you haven't seen my closet yet." She threw open the door to a junior-sized room, filled with shelves of boxes, groups of skirts and blouses, dresses, jackets, and every kind of clothing.

"It looks like a little department store."

"Let's go to your room," Mary said as I gawked at the closet. Next door was a smaller version of Mary's room, and there was a crucifix over its bed, too.

"Why don't you unpack? I'll be through in the bathroom in a few minutes."

It didn't take me long to hang up my blouse and skirt for tomorrow in the big closet. I slipped my pajamas under the pillow and put my hairbrush on the dresser. I was glad to be able to stretch out on the bed. I was almost asleep when Mary called out that the bathroom was mine.

I splashed cold water on my face, and after I combed my hair, I felt better.

We could hear voices as we walked down the stairs.

"That's my Aunt Irene." Two women were standing near the fireplace, engrossed in a conversation. Mary introduced me first to her mother, a tall, slim woman with stylishly waved hair and a smooth face.

"How do you do, Deborah? I am so glad you could come." She looked at the watch hanging from her blouse. "Will you excuse me? I must dress."

If Mrs. Regan was formal, Aunt Irene was not. She took both my hands in hers and squeezed them warmly.

"So you're going to do Yum-Yum? How exciting." She nodded her head slowly. "You could look the part without any trouble. After dinner, we'll get to work and I'll give you all my secrets." Her wink and her dimpled, broad smile enchanted me and left me feeling I'd like to know her better.

When Mrs. Regan returned, wearing a fresh, blue dress, we walked into the brightly lit dining room. The table was set with ruby goblets and several kinds of forks, spoons, and knives. On each plate was a porcelain ring holding a cloth napkin.

Why so much flatware on the table? At home, we had one of each kind. How would I know which one to use? I wondered, as I was seated between Mary and Aunt Irene, facing Mr. and Mrs. Regan.

Mrs. O'Rourke brought in platters of vegetables and boiled potatoes sprinkled with parsley and placed them on the table. Then she came around to each of us with the fish.

I took a little of each dish. Now I had to make a decision. I reasoned that since the smaller fork was first it was meant to be used first. I picked it up, intending to spear a small piece of fish, when Aunt Irene turned to me.

"Mary tells me you have four brothers, Debbie."

I put my fork down. "That's right." I told them about my family. By now, I could see that everyone was using the larger fork, and I followed suit. All I had to do was to watch.

The bread looked delicious. I put a slice on my plate but first buttered it, being careful to use the smallest knife. I was congratulating myself when I observed Mrs. Regan breaking off a small piece of bread before she buttered it. I was halfway through my slice of bread by then so I just finished it.

Aunt Irene and Mr. Regan were having an interesting conversation. Mr. Regan was talking about the differences between President Wilson and President Harding. He had so much to say about our past president. It was an eye-opener for me.

I relaxed. I could eat all of the food that was served. I was enjoying my dinner when I suddenly realized that the Regans' dishes had probably been used to hold pork. Jewish people are not allowed to eat bacon or ham or any pork product. At home, Mama had different sets of dishes for meat and for dairy, in keeping with kosher.

Just then the pain in my side returned and my stomach did a somersault. Mumbling an excuse, I scraped my chair back and fled up the stairs to the bathroom. I got there not a minute too soon. I cleaned up and hoped the smell of vomit would go away.

There was a knock on the door, and Mary asked how I felt. She looked worried when I came out, so I told her about the pain in my side and what had happened in the gym.

"That sure was bad aim on Jenny's part," Mary said.

Since Jenny was her friend, I didn't tell her about my suspicions. Back in the dining room, I apologized, but Mary explained how I was feeling.

"Will you be able to sing tonight, Debbie?" Aunt Irene asked.

"Yes, I'm feeling much better, really."

We went into the parlor and sat at the piano together. Aunt Irene sang for me, and then I sang for her.

"Debbie, you have a good voice, a true voice. Not a strong one, but for that you would have to work hard."

"That's just what Mr. Desser tells me."

"Who is Mr. Desser?"

I told her about my lessons with him at the Bronx Settlement House.

"Good. Are you interested in becoming a singer?"

I took a deep breath. "I think so."

"Well, I promised you some tips on playing Yum-Yum. First, I want to show you something I've brought from my personal collection."

She unwrapped a little fan. Slim, black veins held together a picture of a Japanese lady standing on a bridge.

Aunt Irene opened the fan. "Now watch what you can do."

With a flick of her wrist, she quickly closed the fan and opened it again.

"When you want to show agitation, fan yourself with short, vigorous strokes."

"I had no idea that fans could be used that way."

"Yes, my dear. Now if you want to flirt, then hide your face behind the fan — like this."

It was a wonderful hour, not only because of the clever things Aunt Irene showed me, or because she was so encouraging about my voice. It was Aunt Irene herself. She brought the magic of the stage right to me, and I loved every minute of it.

Then Mary joined us, and I flopped happily into one of the armchairs. Mary put a record on the Victrola while Aunt Irene thumbed through a magazine. It felt good to relax.

"Debbie, how would you like some milk and cake?" Since there was no food in my stomach, I told Mary I'd love it.

Soon it was time for bed. In the bedroom, I undressed in front of the dresser mirror, a luxury I never had at home. Without a stitch of clothing on, I studied my naked body, and it gave me pleasure to see my breasts and rounded hips. For some reason, I was thinking about Ben when I slipped into my new pink pajamas.

I was giving my hair its one hundred strokes when Mary swept in, wearing a long, frilly nightgown and bunny slippers.

"Still giving it the one hundred strokes every night? That's old-fashioned. Why don't you get your hair bobbed?" She shook her head in the freedom that short hair gave her.

"I have to convince my mother first."

"Oh, mothers. Sometimes the less they know, the better. Can you keep a secret? I want to show you something my brother brought back from college for me this past Christmas. If my mother knew it, she'd be very angry."

When Mary returned she had a small, flat silver bottle in her hand.

"What is it?"

"It's a flask. It's the latest thing to take along on dates."

"What do you put into it?"

"You are an innocent, Debbie. Whiskey, of course. It's better than going to a speakeasy."

I wasn't going to show my ignorance again. Maybe Davy would know what a speakeasy was. So I said nothing.

"See you early in the morning." Mary yawned her good night.

I was exhausted, but I couldn't fall asleep. My eyes kept opening, straining in the dark to see the crucifix over my head. Finally I pulled the blanket out and put the pillow at the foot of the bed. Now at least I could keep my eyes shut.

It was quiet without the boys tumbling about like cubs on the other side of my curtain. And it felt queer not to have anyone to say good night to — just the clock ticking away. Somehow, as I lay there in the dark, the pain in my side and the ticking of the clock seemed to join hands.

14

THERE WAS a knock at the door.

"Rise and shine, Debbie. Rise and shine!"

It was an effort to open my eyes. For a moment, I didn't know who was calling or where in the world I was. Then the little crucifix came into focus and the whole thing flooded back.

Just a moment, Mary," I called, quickly rearranging the bed.

"Come in."

She was wearing a cuddly robe. "How are you feeling?"

"Not bad." I moved somewhat gingerly, surprised at the tenderness in my right side. I slipped into my skirt and blouse as quickly as I could and joined Mary.

We tiptoed down the stairs through the quiet house and stopped at the library.

"Dad promised to pull out some books that we could use," Mary said.

I walked slowly around the book-lined walls, reading the titles. There were whole shelves of books on Shakespeare, Dickens, and so many others. I enjoyed touching their leather bindings. I could have spent hours in this room, but Mary was impatient.

We looked at the books her father had left on the desk with a note: "Hope these help with Patrick. Good luck. Dad."

Dad! The word sounded so good to me that I rolled it silently around in my mouth. How would it be to call Papa by such an American name as Dad? I wondered, as we walked downstairs to have breakfast.

The kitchen, a huge room with a long table in the middle, was big enough to fit the whole Gold flat into it.

"I'm making breakfast this morning. Tillie isn't here today."

"Just a glass of milk and some toast, please."

"Are you keeping your girlish figure or is it your stomach?"

"A little of both."

We were almost finished with our breakfast when Aunt Irene appeared, dressed in her coat and hat. She looked intently at me. "I have come to give you something." She held out the little fan. "This is for you."

I couldn't believe it. "You want me to have it?"

"Yes. Cherish it, and I know it will help you be a real Yum-Yum on Thursday." Then she hugged me and turned to embrace her niece. With a wave of her arm, she was off.

"Aunt Irene must really think you're good if she parted with that fan," Mary said.

"It's the nicest thing that's ever happened to me." I meant it. I was touched by the precious little gift.

"Let's get going on our report. Remember, there's a medal for us if it's a winner."

"Just let me put my fan in my room and I'll meet you in a few minutes."

The rest of the day we concentrated on Patrick Henry. It was a joy to work in that library. Mr. Regan came in once, looking freshly shaved and handsome. He took time to tell me about the books and had a lot more to say, but Mary shooed him out.

The only other interruption was from Mrs. Regan. "I'm on my way out and I just wanted to say how glad I am to have met you, Debbie. I hope you have a huge success Thursday in *The Mikado*."

"Your mother's a beautiful woman, Mary."

"You think so? You should see her daughter."

The pain in my side was making me edgy, and I was

happy to stop and stretch, although we didn't want to waste too much time. When the last "t" was crossed and all the "i's" were dotted, I heaved a big sigh of relief.

"Am I glad this is finished!"

"Me, too. How would you like to visit Jane Simmons this afternoon?"

"I think I'd better get home, Mary."

"In that case, I'll ask Dad to drop you off first, and I'll go on to Jane's."

"Good. I'll be packed in a few minutes."

Despite the pain in my side, I sat back in the car, happy that the report and the little fan were safe in the carpetbag resting at my feet. The car drew up to my house and Mr. Regan came around to open the door.

"Debbie, good luck on Thursday. I have an idea there will be great reviews for your performance." He smiled at me. "Shall I carry the bag for you?"

"Thank you, Mr. Regan. Thank you for everything. I'll manage the bag myself." If he carried it up, it would only be polite to invite him in and somehow today was not the day.

I walked up the stairs slowly, the bag getting heavier by the second. Finally, I plopped it down in front of apartment 3G. Inside I could hear dishes rattling, so I knew my family was eating dinner. The smell of food and the heat rushed at me when I opened the door. Everybody crowded around and started asking questions.

"Come sit," Mama scolded. "Everything is getting cold. She can talk at the table."

I must have answered a hundred questions before everything closed in. My head was swimming and I fought back the impulse to cry. Instead I found myself scolding Michael.

"Why don't you wipe that disgusting-looking milk from your face?"

"Sure thing," he said good-naturedly, and wiped his mouth with the back of his hand.

"Mama, why can't we have napkins on the table when we eat?"

"Hoity-toity lady," Michael mimicked me in a high falsetto voice.

"Don't be disgusting. People are not supposed to eat like animals."

"Molly, Debbie is right," Papa said. "How come we don't have napkins?"

"On Friday nights we do, when there is a tablecloth and candles."

"But, Mama, we should have them every night."

"What about the laundry?" Davy asked.

"That's easy," Michael said. "Come on, Elliot. We'll be back in a moment." They returned with seven folded squares of toilet paper, which they distributed with such aplomb that even I had to laugh.

Before I could explain how cloth napkins could be used several times by having a napkin holder, a wave of nausea engulfed me. I had to put my head down on the table.

There was absolute silence and then I heard Mama say, "From eating non-kosher food, what could you expect?"

I wanted to tell Mama how wrong she was. But the lump in my stomach suddenly lurched up, and I was retching into something mercifully held under my chin.

At last I was in my own bed, with cool, clean sheets against my hot body. The pain had become so excruciating that I knew it must be the time for me to die.

I don't know how much later it was when Dr. Ferber was sitting on my bed, questioning, probing, and pushing. From a distance, I could hear voices: "hospital...appendix... emergency." Then David was carrying me into a car, Dr. Ferber's, I guessed. My head was on Mama's lap. But why was she telling Papa in a low voice that he must go to see Uncle Pincus for money? Mama knew how Papa hated to ask Uncle Pincus for anything.

I lifted my head to tell Mama that the first performance of *The Mikado* was this Thursday. Wherever they were taking me, I had to be back by then. I wasn't making myself understood, because Mama shushed me and patted my head.

"Don't worry your *keppele*, Debbie."

My keppele? There's nothing wrong with my head, I wanted to say to Mama. And there was Aunt Irene's fan. It had to be handled carefully because it was so old.

But someone in white took over and I remembered no more.

15

From a distant place I heard a voice repeating over and over, "How are you, Deborah? How are you?"

I pulled my eyes open. A woman with a funny, pie-shaped hat was bending over me.

"How are you feeling? Do you know your name?"

"My name? My name is Deborah Gold. I'm all right, I guess."

Was that my voice? It seemed so thin and far away. Under the covers, my hand explored the bandages around my body.

"Where am I?"

"You are in the hospital. Your appendix was removed, and I must say, you were a very sick girl."

I shut my eyes again and let the waves of weariness roll over me. The nurse said something about parents and disappeared. I would have slipped back to sleep, but a strong voice on my right jarred me awake.

"I'm Mrs. Fanelli," it called out. "Your mother and father have been waiting all day to see you."

I didn't open my eyes, but the voice continued. "I had my appendix out last week. I'm feeling good now, and next week I'll be going home."

Before I could ask the voice what day of the week it was, Mama and Papa were walking toward me. They sat by my bed, one on each side. Mama kissed me on the forehead and Papa stroked my hand.

"How do you feel, Debbie?"

"Papa, what day of the week is it?"

"Now, Debbie, don't excite yourself."

With all my strength, I asked again. "Just tell me what day it is. Please!"

Papa looked at Mama. "It's Monday." Why couldn't he have said so immediately? I lay back in relief.

"I made soup special for you," Mama murmured. She unpacked a bowl of chicken soup and began to spoon-feed me. Automatically I opened my mouth and swallowed.

Something the voice on the right had said still disturbed me. What was it? Suddenly I remembered, and I pushed the spoon away from my mouth, spilling some of the soup on my gown.

"The lady said she had her operation last week and she will be going home next week. How long do I have to be here?"

They said nothing. Then Papa looked at Mama and she nodded to him.

"You know, Debbie, you were very sick. You still are."

"Papa, just tell me how long I'll be in the hospital."

Papa looked at Mama. "Maybe two weeks," she said.

"Two weeks!" I pushed my fist into my mouth and muffled the wail that rose from deep inside me.

"Debbie, Debbie, you'll make yourself more trouble."

The nurse with the pie-shaped hat was bending over me, a pill in her hand. "Swallow this."

Between sobs I gulped it down with a sip of water. And then I floated off and away, with someone crying, crying....

I was running on a strip of beach — dark, swirling waters on either side, bare land, no trees, no rocks. No place to hide from the monster bird that kept swooping down at me, its sharp claws and cruel beak poised to tear me to pieces.

Across the water, there was a jut of land with rocks and trees where I could hide from the monster bird. I had no choice, so I flung myself into the icy, black waters, which sucked me down again and again until, choking and coughing, I was thrown onto the beach. I dragged myself to a tree, safe at last.

It was warm and sunny there, with singing birds in all the trees. If only the voices would stop calling me. They kept waking me up. If only they would leave me alone—I just wanted to sleep. I ate automatically so I could return once more to my distant land.

When I was awake, I could only think about Jenny Sharp and what she'd done to me. The thoughts hurt. One day I awoke to find Dr. Ferber sitting on my bed. He took my wrist in his hand.

"Debbie, what's wrong? Something's troubling you."

I said nothing.

"Is it because you missed *The Mikado*?"

"No and yes."

"What do you mean?"

"Well, I couldn't do the show because...because a person wanted me to miss it."

"How could that be?"

"There's this girl. She was very angry at me." I explained what had happened.

"You mean she deliberately hit you with that big ball?"

"I believe so."

"Then listen to me, Debbie." He put his hand on my shoulder. "No matter how hard that ball smashed into you, it did not give you your appendicitis. That is my medical opinion."

"You're sure, Dr. Ferber, that the ball did not put me in the hospital?" I wanted to hear him say it again.

"Positive."

He looked at me so kindly I knew he was my friend, and I believed him. After he left, I fell asleep, but it was a lighter, more restful sleep.

And when I felt a gentle pull on my hand, I opened my eyes and was looking up at Iz Berg.

"Hi, Iz. What day of the week is it?"

"Friday. You look better, Debbie."

"Friday! Then it was yesterday..."

He nodded. "We sure missed you."

I couldn't help the tears. "Who did Yum-Yum?"

"Your understudy, Betty. She was all right, but you would have been great!"

"Tell me everything that happened, Iz. Don't leave anything out."

"Let's get you comfortable first." He propped the pillows against my back. There was an unfinished glass of milk on the table. "And drink this. Here I go."

He launched into a blow-by-blow description of what had happened. Someone tripped over her robe, and the curtain came down too fast. He was funny and I laughed and laughed.

"It's good to hear you laugh." And now he looked serious. "You see, I was worried about you. My father," Iz was looking out into space, "my father died from appendicitis. The trouble was...we couldn't afford a doctor, and so he waited until it was too late.

"That's why I just have to be a doctor, Debbie." For a second, his thin face was drawn into a solemn look as if he were taking an oath. And then he was himself again. "Before I forget, this envelope is from the cast. I have to leave now."

Before I could open the large, bulging envelope, the woman on my right was saying, "It's nice you are feeling better. Your Mama will be happy to see you awake. All the time you were sleeping."

I turned to see a large woman with thick, black hair and a friendly face. She was munching on a cracker. "Here — have one."

I was hungry, so I reached across. I wondered what kind of cracker could taste so good.

"That's a nice boyfriend you have."

"Boyfriend? Oh, you mean Iz?"

"Sure, he was here almost every day."

"Really? He's just a good friend."

Had Ben come, too? I wondered. Perhaps there was a note from him in the envelope. Eagerly I dumped the letters and cards on my lap and opened some of them. The one from Jenny I read carefully. She was sorry about my being in the hospital and missing *The Mikado*. And she felt so bad about the accident in the gym. She hoped there was no connection.

I wondered if I should let her sweat about it or tell her what Dr. Ferber said. I thumbed quickly through the rest of the letters and cards. There was nothing from Ben. Could he have stopped in like Iz had done and I didn't know about it?

It wasn't until my parents came to visit that I found out Ben had not forgotten me. Mama came in, relief written all over her face. "Oy, already you look better."

Then she remembered the package in the drawer of the table beside my bed. "This came for you yesterday."

It was from Ben. I smoothed the small package and carefully untied the string. It was a little book with a strange-sounding name, the *Rubaiyat of Omar Khayyam* — a book of love poems.

16

ONCE I BEGAN to mend, I could appreciate all the attention I was getting. The biggest thrill was receiving a bouquet of flowers from the cast and Miss Beck.

There was a constant stream of visitors, and my aunts and uncles brought gifts. Aunt Becky's cuddly, blue bathrobe was the best. The day I knew Ben was coming, I slipped into it and put a matching blue ribbon in my hair.

"You look real cute," Mrs. Fanelli said.

"Thank you." I checked my hair for the tenth time in the new tortoise-shell hand mirror that Mary Regan had brought from her family and Aunt Irene.

"Very sweet indeed," said Mrs. Oliver, who occupied the third bed.

We three had become good friends. I felt as if I'd known them all my life. Mrs. Fanelli and I worried about little Mrs. Oliver. She had a broken hip that was taking a long time to mend. Silver-haired and fragile, Mrs. Oliver ate like a sparrow.

At mealtimes, Mrs. Fanelli would throw up her hands and scold, "Mrs. Oliver, how can you get better if you don't eat?"

Mrs. Fanelli was forever urging someone to eat her homemade goodies, but Mrs. Oliver refused everything. No one had come to visit her in the month she'd been in the hospital, and she was lonely. Sometimes she spoke about her daughter, who was supposed to come but had never shown up. We wondered if there really was such a person.

My visitor was real. When Ben walked through the doorway, looking so handsome in his tan jacket, I was filled with joy. He bent over to give me a little kiss on the lips. I could feel my face flush.

"You look great," he said.

"I feel better now."

"Did you get the book I sent you?"

"Yes, and I've been reading some of the poems. Do you know them?"

"To be honest, no, but my mother thought you might enjoy them. Perhaps you'll lend the book to me."

"Did you know they were love poems?" He nodded.

"That's why I sent them."

It was good that he'd come early and we had a few minutes alone. Between Mrs. Fanelli and me, the room filled quickly with visitors. He squeezed my hand to say good-bye and left.

Later in the week, Papa came in carrying a large, flat carton. "Debbie," Papa panted, "just wait until you open this and see what's inside for you."

"I haven't seen you all week, Papa. Mama said you were working late every night. Are you feeling all right?" He looked tired and pale.

"Never mind me," Papa chuckled. "Just open the box."

I tried to undo the knotted string, but Papa finally did it for me. When I removed the top of the box, a lovely whiff of new fabric tickled my nose. I gently lifted something green and soft out of the carton.

"Papa," I gasped, "a store-bought coat. Is it…is it for me?"

"For who else, silly? Ask me how it got made. Go ahead, ask me."

The coat was belted and had a double row of buttons. The beautiful, emerald-green cloth was as soft as a cloud.

Papa was so excited he couldn't wait. "It's a lunch-hour coat!"

"What's a lunch-hour coat?"

Papa twinkled and grinned from ear to ear. "Good that

you ask. You see, since the strike the men have become friendly. So when I told them how you missed *The Mikado*, they wanted to help do something for you.

"First, we got permission from the foreman to make the coat. The material was a remnant. For leftover pieces from the ladies' coats you get a bargain."

Papa continued the story with great relish. "Now comes the good part. Morris, the pattern maker, cut the coat during his lunch hour. Then I sewed it during my lunch hours. And yesterday another friend used his lunch hour to finish and press the coat. It's beautiful, isn't it?"

"How can I thank everybody?"

"Maybe you should write a little letter."

"I will. I will."

And then I asked Papa what had been on my mind since that night in Dr. Ferber's car, when I'd heard Mama tell Papa to ask Pincus for money. "Papa, did you have to get Uncle Pincus to loan you money to pay the bills for the hospital?"

There was a sad look in Papa's eyes. "That's not your problem. You just get well and come home. Money is for fathers to worry about," he said and began coughing.

When the coughing spasm stopped, I told him about my visit to the Regans. There were so few times I had Papa to myself, and there was so much to share with him.

"And you know, Papa, I was going to call you Dad. Doesn't that sound American? Dad."

"Dad," Papa repeated and shrugged his shoulders. Then he laughed. "There's a man in my shop goes to night school. One day, he told us about this writer who said that no matter what you call a rose, it still smells like a rose. So call me what you like. I'm still Papa."

"You know, I think that comes from *Romeo and Juliet*. We're studying Shakespeare this term."

"Shakespeare? He lived a long time ago, didn't he?"

"I think four hundred years ago."

"Imagine — a man writes something and four hundred

years later people are still saying what he wrote." Papa looked wistful. "Someday, if I would have the time to read this Shakespeare..."

Papa stayed until the food trays were brought in, and then he left, the clumsy box under one arm. My eyes followed him. When had Papa gotten so short and small, with such stooped shoulders? Only yesterday I thought he was the tallest, handsomest man in the world. Is this what growing up meant — you got big and your father shrank?

But Mrs. Fanelli and Mrs. Oliver wanted to hear all about the coat, so I shared the lunch-hour story with them while we ate. That is, while Mrs. Fanelli and I went through our supper with relish and Mrs. Oliver picked at her food.

"How are you going to get better if you don't eat?" Mrs. Fanelli scolded. "If I ate like you, I'd fade away."

Jolly Miss Spark, the night nurse, came in to remove the trays and plump up our pillows. "Are you ready for your company?" she asked.

When I was finished using my tortoise-shell hand mirror, I offered it to Mrs. Oliver. I think she knew how proud I was of this gift. She thanked me and fixed her hair a bit, although she had no interest in looking pretty since she had no visitors. She was too polite to turn down my new mirror.

While Mrs. Oliver was arranging her hair, Miss Spark appeared in the doorway with a young woman who I knew immediately was Mrs. Oliver's daughter. They had the same small frame and delicate features. Then I noticed the blank look in the woman's eyes and the cane in her hand.

"Marsha, I'm here!" Mrs. Oliver called out with a ring of joy in her voice. Miss Spark led the blind woman to her mother. They embraced and held on to each other for a long while.

The day before I was supposed to go home, Aunt Becky stopped in to see me. Her cheeks were flushed and her eyes were dancing.

"Debbie, before your mama comes, I have a secret to tell

you." She took a deep breath. "John and I are going to be married tomorrow by a justice of the peace in a courtroom."

"Aunt Becky!" I hugged her. "How wonderful! I'm going to love having John as my uncle."

"If only everybody felt that way. You know, I haven't told my sisters." A shadow passed over the bright face. "I'm hoping that after I'm married and they meet him, he'll be accepted in the family."

"Everybody will love him," I assured her.

"I pray you are right. One more kiss for good luck and then I'm off. Remember, don't say anything about this to anyone. I will send each of my sisters a telegram."

After that, I couldn't wait to get home. The pain at missing *The Mikado* was deep. But there was so much ahead of me: Aunt Becky's wedding, Ben Stein, graduation in a few months, and then — Jefferson High School, here I come!

17

How good it felt to come home. It was on a Friday morning, the day Mama took the house apart, yet I couldn't believe how much I'd missed each crowded room. Only the bombshell of the telegram Aunt Becky would send hung over my head.

"Sure beats the hospital bed," I said, bouncing on my feather quilt.

Had I been missed? Donny, so sweet and warm, refused to leave my bed. He kept putting wet, smoochy Donny kisses all over me.

"I love you, too, Donny baby," I breathed into his sweet-smelling neck. We played and he showed me all his new tricks until he fell asleep.

A few minutes after three, Michael and Elliot rushed in. "We ran all the way home," they announced, their black eyes shining.

Michael grabbed me around the neck in a bear hug. Elliot stood off until I held my arms out to him.

"You don't have to scrub the floor today," Elliot whispered in my ear. "We're going to do it for you."

And they did, Mama came in later to report. "You should see, the boys cleaned the floor." And then she surprised me, because Mama rarely complimented her children. "Not as good as you do."

That wasn't the only surprise. I wanted to put Aunt Irene's fan in my secret box underneath the bed, so I pulled it out. A note was attached to the box: "We don't touch sick people's things. Your brothers."

At sunset, with everybody home, I put on my new robe and walked into the dim Sabbath kitchen. The delicate fragrance of fresh greens simmering in chicken broth hung in the warm air and mingled with the yeasty scent of cooling coffee cake.

It was as if I were seeing everything for the very first time. Mama had already dropped a coin into the *pishke*, her charity box. We heard the plink just before she lit the Sabbath candles.

Mama had put on her white, lacy headcloth. As I watched, her fingers touched each candle and there was light — three glowing heads on three white stalks. The rosy flames reached into the shadows of the kitchen, gleaming and dancing around the room, on the glass doors of the cupboards, on the shiny linoleum floor. Mama's hands circled the candles three times and then she covered her face with her hands. I could hear her say the *Baruch Atah*, Blessed Art Thou. Then Mama was silent and I knew she was adding her own prayers. Tonight I must have been included, because the first thing she did when she removed her hands was look at me.

"*Gut Shabbes*," Mama said, folding her headcloth.

"Gut Shabbes, Mama," we answered.

I'd come home at long last from a strange, hard journey.

Around the snowy-white tablecloth we sat and waited for Papa to serve the twisted golden *challa*, the bread baked for the Sabbath meal. He lifted it up, said a prayer over it, then broke off a small piece for each one of us.

"It's good to have another woman in the house," he said, handing me the first piece.

Everybody was in a gay mood. Papa told his best stories about Mr. Gittelman, who worked in Papa's shop. Every kind of funny misfortune happened to Mr. Gittelman, Papa's favorite *schlimazel*.

I didn't feel like talking with so much good food to eat.

There was Mama's gefilte fish with horseradish, her home-made noodles floating in hot soup, her roasted chicken, and my favorite, *tsimmes*, a tasty combination of carrots, sweet potatoes, and prunes. I waited for dessert with a groaning stomach.

"It looks like they starve you patients in the hospital," Papa said, smiling.

"Not really, Papa," I mumbled, my mouth full of strudel. "It just doesn't taste like Mama's food."

The next day, a parade of neighbors and friends came to visit and kept Mama busy serving tea and homemade cookies. But every time I heard a knock, I held my breath. Was it the telegram from Aunt Becky? What if my family would not accept Aunt Becky's marriage to John O'Neill? What if they declared her dead? I quickly brushed the thought out of my head.

How could I live without my aunt? Who could I turn to when I had a problem or a puzzling question? Just last summer before my thirteenth birthday, when I was expecting the big event of my life, Aunt Becky had once again proved her worth.

All I knew was what I'd heard from girls in school. It was called "the curse," or "the monthly," or by some, "my period." When Esther and I talked about it, we found out that neither of us knew much.

Aunt Becky had explained it simply, and for the first time in my life I heard the word "menstruation." But Aunt Becky did not prepare me for the funny thing that happened when it finally showed and I told Mama about it. She smacked me sharply on one cheek and then the other.

"Why, Mama?" I had stammered, holding my red face. "That's what my mother did to me," she explained. "It's to make sure you always have color in your cheeks."

Then Mama brought out an old, torn bedsheet that she must have been saving for this occasion and stripped it into napkins for me. I would have to do a lot of washing to make this small supply last.

"Debbie, is there anything you want to know?" Mama asked in a strained voice. She looked relieved when I shook my head.

The telegram finally arrived on Sunday morning. Mama was up early and answered the door. She stood pale and frightened, the unopened envelope in her hand.

"Max, a telegram! Who would send us a telegram?"

Papa opened it and read aloud in a shaky voice: "Married to John O'Neill. Please share our happiness. Love, Becky."

Mama sat down. "Love, Becky? What does it mean?"

"It says she is married to John O'Neill."

"She is married?"

"Yes, Mama. Aunt Becky married John O'Neill," I said, adding quickly, "it says in the telegram."

"O'Neill? O'Neill? That's a Jewish name?"

Papa shook his head. Then Mama did what I'd never seen her do before. She put her head on the table and cried.

The crying turned into bedlam as each aunt arrived carrying an identical telegram. Aunt Rosie, usually so careful with her dress, was wearing an unpressed blouse. Aunt Sadie sailed into the kitchen with her hair flying in all directions.

Last to arrive were Aunt Yetta, looking pale, and Uncle Pincus, red-faced and angry. He slammed his telegram on the table and shouted, "We don't have a sister, Rebecca. We will sit shivah for a Rebecca O'Neill."

At the word "shivah," a mourning period for the dead, such a wail arose from the sisters that Donny screamed and Mama had to comfort him.

"Mama, I'll take Donny." I held him close to me and whispered in his ear. He stopped screaming. I kissed his chubby cheeks and smoothed back his damp hair.

Uncle Pincus continued shouting. "Anyone who gives up Selig Samuels from Samuels' Dress Manufacturing Company for, for...is no relative of mine!"

"Who is this John . . . John O' . . . what's his name?" Aunt Rosie asked between sobs.

"He's very nice," I whispered into Donny's ear.

"Why couldn't she marry a Jewish man?" Aunt Yetta kept repeating.

"She loves John O'Neill, that's why," I whispered in the baby's other ear.

"This, this what's-his-name," Uncle Pincus was saying with bitter hatred in his voice, "what is he? A street cleaner?"

Before I could stop myself, I'd blurted out, "Street cleaner! He is not! He's just the sweetest, dearest person and he is a teacher!"

Stunned silence filled the room. Then Papa asked, "How do you know this?"

I explained about my meeting John, trying to hold back my tears. I had made it worse for Aunt Becky, I was sure.

Uncle Pincus stormed, "So. How do you like that? A thirteen-year-old girl she tells everything. But us she keeps in the dark. I say we have no sister — for us she is dead!"

It was impossible. I set Donny on Mama's lap and rushed out of the room to my bed. I buried my head in the pillow and tried to stifle my sobs. I could only ask myself, why, why, why? Why was it so terrible for a Jewish woman to marry out of her religion?

What did it mean to be a Jew anyhow? Was it Mama lighting the Sabbath candles? Was it the queasy feeling I had in the hospital when I was served a ham dinner by mistake?

Or was it listening to my relatives tell horrible stories about pogroms in the Old Country and how innocent people were murdered just because they were Jews?

It was all too much for me. I broke down and sobbed. Suddenly I felt a gentle hand on my shoulders.

It was Papa. "Don't carry on like this, Debbie."

"I can't understand why Aunt Becky's marriage is so terrible." I turned to look at him. "It's ridiculous. How could she be dead to us? You don't even know John."

"Debbie, I know it's hard for you to understand. You see, Jewish people are scattered over the whole world. Only their religion makes them one people. Compared to the rest of the world, there are very few Jews. What would happen if intermarriage were allowed?"

I said nothing, and Papa continued. "Soon there would be fewer and fewer Jews in the world. Eventually, we would be no more."

Papa's explanation did not console me. Not to see Aunt Becky anymore? She was more like a sister to me than an aunt, and I'd always longed for a sister. I was miserable.

Later, when the angry shouting and crying no longer stormed around in my head, I tried to sleep but couldn't stop sobbing. There was no way I could live without Aunt Becky, no way. I tossed and turned until I felt raw and numb. I hugged myself to make the pain go away.

My hand wandered over my body. I remembered the teacher, back in the fourth grade, showing us a special map. She made us shut our eyes and feel with our fingers the height of the Rocky Mountains, the flat plains, and the rivers. So it was with me. I discovered my new land, and it was warm and comforting.

18

THE GLOOM in the house grew heavier in the next few days as my aunts and uncles discussed the formal grieving for Aunt Becky. Uncle Pincus was certain that shivah was the only choice, but Mama for once opposed her brother-in-law.

"I'm the oldest in the family," Mama said. "I was responsible for her coming to America and encouraging her to go to school." Mama shook her head. "There is a rabbi on the East Side of Manhattan. He can help us decide what to do. But now, we have to get ready for Passover."

Of all the Jewish holidays, Passover was my favorite. Although I looked forward to it this spring, the chance that my family would consider Aunt Becky dead still gave me nightmares.

When Esther, wanting to cheer me up, suggested we go see the newest Rudolph Valentino movie, I was delighted. It had been some time since we'd gone out together. My new friends were exciting, I decided, as we walked to the movies, but being with Esther was like putting on comfortable old slippers.

"Es," I said, trying to make her understand how I felt about her, "even though I haven't been able to spend much time with you lately, just knowing you are next door is..." I shook my head, unable to put it into words as we walked arm in arm.

Instead, I found it easier to describe my visit to Mary's house. "I think they live in another world," I concluded.

Esther, always practical, said, "It's nice to know how she lives, but how would it be if you invited her to your house?"

I sighed, "I've thought about that. I'd like to invite her, but what would she think of our flat? It could fit into her kitchen."

Esther shrugged her shoulders. "Well, I think you should invite her anyway, or maybe just stick to your old friends."

"I'll always stick to my special old friends." I squeezed her arm.

An unexpected opportunity turned up at the supper table that night when David spoke about the coming Passover *Seder*.

"Mama, did you know that, according to tradition, you're supposed to invite a guest to the Seder?"

"Then how would it be if I invited Mary Regan?" I asked, without giving myself a chance to think about it.

"Mary Regan?" Mama was frowning. "How could we invite Mary Regan?"

"Mama," David said, "Debbie should be allowed to invite her friend. It's the tradition." Because it was her David who had suggested it, Mama could do no more than throw up her hands and say, "So invite."

Within the hour, the invitation was on its way. Two days later, a letter arrived, saying how pleased Mary would be to come to the Seder. I was both elated and worried.

Papa had some comforting words. "She knows where we live, so she knows what to expect. And for this holiday, the house will shine. The Seder speaks for itself."

He was right about the house. If we cleaned weekly for the Sabbath, for Passover the walls, the windows, the shelves — everything had to be scrubbed. In addition, special pots and dishes, used only for the eight days of Passover, were taken down from the closet. Some of the dishes were like old friends I could only visit once a year. I was particularly fond of a chipped pink serving dish, and when that dish appeared on the table, I knew it was Passover.

It was a holiday with special foods. Papa had already

made the wine, and Mama filled the kitchen with the smell of onions cooking in chicken fat. *Borsht*, or beet soup, was finishing in a vat under the sink.

The night before Passover was a fun ritual. The house was darkened and Mama lit a candle for us to look for the ten bread crumbs (the *leaven*) she had hidden. Elliot carried the feather to sweep the crumbs, while Michael had a wooden spoon to catch them and drop them into the paper bag.

When the twins counted nine crumbs and couldn't find the tenth, they looked at Mama. "I put one on Donny's tray," she remembered. They looked at the tray, but there was no crumb there. Sitting in his high chair, Donny made "all gone" with his hands.

The twins began to argue over who would say the ritual speech, but Papa stopped them. "Both of you can say it."

So together they said, "If there are any bread crumbs that I have not seen, let them be as nothing, as dust of the earth."

The next morning Mama burnt the feather, the spoon, and the paper bag in the stove.

Then came the Seder. With Mary coming, I wanted the table to look special, hoping she wouldn't notice how it was crowded between the china closet and the piano. Mama had laid out her rarely used white linen tablecloth and matching napkins. A wine glass and a *Haggadah*, the book that tells the order of the Seder, were at each plate. The twins had polished the brass candlesticks and they had never shone brighter. The ceremonial dishes were already in place on the table when Michael, the lookout, announced that the Maxwell had arrived.

"May I go down?" he asked.

"I've already asked David."

I turned and checked my family. Mama, in her new starched apron, and Papa, slim in his blue shirt, tie, and vest, made a pretty nice-looking couple, I thought. The boys were clean, and Donny had a blue bib that matched his eyes and set off his hair.

I took a deep breath and opened the door. Mary and I smiled at each other and hugged.

"It's so good to see you," she said. Then she turned to meet my family. To Mama she handed a small bunch of fresh flowers. Mama looked pleased when she unwrapped them and put them in a jar of water.

Unable to wait for a formal introduction, Michael told Mary that he and Elliot were identical twins.

"I could see that. I've heard about you boys, you know," she said with a big grin on her face.

When we moved to Donny, she asked if she could hold him. "Debbie," she whispered into his neck, "he is so delicious."

Looking at the bliss on her face, I realized that Mary with her wealth didn't have something I had. I, too, was rich — rich with brothers.

Before we sat down at the Seder table, Papa asked Mary if she knew anything about the Passover.

"I do, Mr. Gold. First, my father made me read the Book of Exodus."

"So you know that Moses convinced the Pharaoh to let the Hebrew slaves go." Papa was pleased.

Mary nodded. "Then my father spoke to a Jewish man in his office who gave him a list of foods on the Seder plate. I have the list right here." She pulled it out of her pocketbook and read, "Hard-boiled egg, roasted lamb bone, greens, bitter herbs..."

Papa interrupted her. "We'll be hearing about each one and what it stands for. Each one helps us remember what happened to our people in their fight for freedom."

"I know about the ten plagues that befell the Egyptians," Mary said as we seated ourselves, "but how can that be done at the table?"

"Easy," Michael said. "Should I tell her, Papa?"

"No, no. We'll follow the order in the Haggadah. Remember, Seder means 'the order.' First, Mama lights the candles. Next, we say a blessing, the *Kiddush*, over the wine. Then we have our first sip of wine," he said proudly.

Mama poured water on Papa's hands over a bowl, while David explained that in Temple days, hands were washed before anyone approached the altar.

When it was time for Papa to explain the special Seder plate, on which Mama had put the symbolic foods, he picked up the *karpas*, or green parsley, and handed everyone a piece to be dipped in salt water before eating.

"The salt water," Papa explained, "reminds us of the tears shed by the Jews as slaves, and the green is symbolic of the coming of spring."

Then he uncovered the three matzos, giving half of one to Mama to hide. He held up the remaining matzos, saying that it was the bread our ancestors ate in Egypt.

"And now..." Papa started to say.

"It's our turn," said the twins, their black eyes shining with pride. "We're going to ask the four questions."

Michael read the first one: "Wherefore is this night different from all other nights?" After we read the answer from the Haggadah, Elliot asked the second question.

When the four questions were answered, it was time to do the ten plagues. As each plague was mentioned, we dipped out a drop of wine from the glass to remind us of the Egyptian blood shed in our people's struggle for freedom. It was known as the Lessening of Our Joy ritual.

The singing for *Dayenu* was loud and joyous, only it got Papa coughing, and I said a silent prayer that Papa stay well. So much depended on him. In a choked voice, he asked David to take over for him.

Then David handed each of us a bit of the *maror*, or bitter herb, on a small piece of matzo to remind us that the Egyptians made the lives of our people bitter with slavery. He pointed to the shank bone of the lamb, saying it was to help us remember that when the Angel of Death slew the first-born of the Egyptians, the Lord passed over the homes of our ancestors that were marked with the blood of a lamb.

There were good things to eat from the Passover plate, too. To each of us Papa handed the *charoses*, a delicious combination of chopped apple, nuts, and wine. It represented the clay mixture the slaves used for making bricks. We were starving by then and were also happy to eat the hard-boiled egg dipped in salt water, a reminder of the tears shed.

We knew we were nearing the end, with a good dinner to follow, when Papa filled Elijah's cup with wine and Mama opened the door so Elijah could come in. Elijah is the prophet who will bring us a world of freedom and peace for all. We sang his song, closed the door, and turned to eat the delicious meal Mama had prepared.

Mary had no idea what gefilte fish was, so we explained it was chopped fresh fish made like a hamburger. It tasted great with horseradish. She tried it but liked the soup with matzo balls best.

Mary was the hit of the evening. The twins were smitten with her and Mama hovered over her offering more food, when she wasn't in the kitchen sniffing the fresh flowers. I caught David's eye across the table, and he smiled at me, nodding his head and mouthing the word "tradition."

After dinner Mama nursed Donny, and with the pile of dishes to do in the kitchen, Mary's offer to help surprised me.

"Are you sure?" I asked her.

Mary laughed. "When Tillie takes her days off, I'm the chief bottle washer."

She was good, scraping and organizing the dishes and flatware. I washed while she wiped. It was then she confided to me that she wondered where all of us slept.

Here it comes, I thought, the great divider between our lives. For a moment, I was tempted to make some excuse and not take her into the bedroom, but instead, I asked her to come with me. The door between the dining room and the bedroom had been kept shut on purpose.

"Do you have several bedrooms there?" she asked.

"Just one, Mary, just one," I said, opening the door. "You see, four of us share the room. David sleeps in the single bed at that end, the twins on the big bed, and I sleep behind the curtain."

"You must have thought me a terrible show-off to make a big to-do over the closets in my bedroom," Mary said.

I shook my head. "That was like a dream come true."

"Debbie, I'm going to tell you something." She looked right into my face. "There was a time, if I could have had an arrangement like yours, I'd have given my eyeteeth for it."

Was Mary pulling my leg?

"I'm all right now, of course. But when I was younger and my brother went away to boarding school, I hated to go to sleep. It meant being on a floor all by myself. The fact that my parents were one flight down and Tillie slept one flight up didn't help much. It was scary. If I had known you then, I would have thought you were the luckiest person in the world."

"Thanks for telling me, Mary. But right now, I'd like to have my own room more than anything."

Before Mary's father picked her up, she thanked my parents graciously. I introduced Mr. Regan to the family, and they chatted for a few minutes before the Regans left.

When Mama and I were tidying the kitchen, she told me how nice it was of Mary to bring the flowers. I told her what Mary had said about sharing a bedroom.

"Such a nice girl," Mama said.

"Mama, I'm so glad you like her. And, Mama, I'm sorry I didn't want Mary to visit us before."

All in all, I wrote in my diary, the evening was a great success. I didn't know it was possible to change your thinking in just a few hours.

19

THE GLOW FROM THE SEDER quickly disappeared with the news that my cousin Annie was really moving to Buffalo. But we spent a wonderful day together remembering everything we used to do. From the box underneath my bed we pulled out all our old treasures: the rag dolls we had mothered so much, a broken pince-nez we wore when we played teacher, and the torn scarf we modeled as "mommies." Then we played jacks, and all the old card games.

The best part was having Annie sleep over. We whispered and giggled half the night. In the morning I gave her my present, a thick blue notebook into which I'd carefully copied the love story we were writing. We promised to send each other any new chapters.

I was so gloomy and teary when Annie left that David had to remind me Buffalo was in America and even in the State of New York.

Mary's flowers still had some bloom when I made an important decision.

"Mama, I'd like to get my hair bobbed before I go back to school."

"Bob your hair?" Mama was rushing to meet her sisters to ask the rabbi about Aunt Becky.

"Didn't Mary look nice with her bobbed hair?" I reminded her.

Mama nodded. "Maybe Papa won't like it?"

"Not at first," I thought, since Papa had always called a

woman's hair her crowning glory. Mama shrugged and said nothing. That meant she was letting me decide.

I ran up to Esther's to share my news. She was washing dishes.

"Es, I have so much to tell you."

"I hope it's cheerful," Esther said and turned to face me. Her eyes looked red from crying.

"What happened?"

"What I've known all along is positive now: no Jefferson High for me."

"Oh, Es!"

"I'll be working in Woolworth's part of the week, and then going to Continuation School."

"But you can graduate."

"Probably, but it will take longer. Anyhow, Rome wasn't built in a day and neither is Esther Schein — not the way I'm built. But what's your news?"

"Well, it's good and bad."

I told her about Annie and then about the Seder and Mary. Esther just shook her head.

"But," I went on, "the important news is that I'm getting my hair bobbed tomorrow."

"Are you really going to do that?" Esther was excited. She pulled at the thick hair hanging down her back. "I wish I had the nerve."

"I can't wait to see what you look like," were her parting words.

The next morning I was up early, anxious to get the hair bobbing over with. Trying to control my chattering teeth, I passed the red and white pole and read in the window of the barbershop: "Expert Ladies' Hair Bobbing." The door to the shop opened easily. Facing the mirror was a long row of barber chairs, each with a leather strop for sharpening razors. One wall had shelves of shaving mugs, and the shop reeked of hair tonic.

The place was empty and I could still leave. But at that moment, the curtain in the rear parted, and a short man in a white coat appeared.

"What do you want, Miss?"

"I'd like my hair bobbed."

"Sit here." He put a sheet around my shoulders. All I could see in the mirror was my hair, the hair I had so faithfully brushed and braided. Now it would no longer hang down my back in all its shining glory.

"You sure you wanna cut it?" The sharp scissors were poised in his hand.

"Yes." With my eyes shut, I could hear the harsh shearing sound of the scissors going click, click around my head. When I opened my eyes, all I could see was my naked long neck in the mirror.

The barber sensed my panic. "Don't worry, Miss. A wave will make it look beautiful."

I didn't have the money to get it washed and waved, so I thanked him and paid the bill. I covered my head with a scarf I had thought to bring along.

When I got home, I slinked into the bathroom and got to work with Vaseline and curlers. By the time Papa came home, my hair was shiny and the waves were in place. I felt much better about it.

"My modern daughter," Papa said. There was pride in his voice.

Even Mama liked it now. She offered to help me pick out a dress for tomorrow. But I wanted to do it myself.

After being away for three full weeks, I wanted to make a smashing return. A lot of kids would be greeting me and, of course, Ben would be there.

I picked out a blue cotton dress from last year that had some style to it. After I'd washed and starched the dress I pulled it off the line still damp. I was tempted to ask Mama to iron it for me. No, I shook my head, still not used to the air that flowed around my head instead of hair. I had to do it myself, I decided, even though I'd been known to scorch things.

The two irons heating on the stove frightened me. Gingerly I lifted one hot iron with the iron holder and brought it to the ironing board. If it was too hot, I'd be in trouble. As

Mama always did, I wet my finger, touched it lightly to the bottom, and listened. Was that the right sizzling sound? To make sure, I ironed a scrap of cloth.

With great care, I pressed each part of the dress, replacing the cooled iron with the hot one. When I hung the dress on the hanger, ready for tomorrow, I breathed a sigh of relief.

Though I planned to get a good night's sleep, I had too much on my mind. I tossed and turned, worried about Aunt Becky.

The family's decision about Aunt Becky was both good and bad. The rabbi agreed it wasn't necessary to declare Becky dead. But to make peace with Uncle Pincus, the sisters promised not to have anything to do with her. She and her husband were to be family outcasts.

And wasn't Esther's news just as bad? While I didn't know for sure where I'd be this fall, Esther did. If I went to Jefferson, we'd be separated, making new friends and having new experiences without each other.

Of course, if I didn't go to Jefferson, it would be disaster for me, too. It would probably be the end of Ben Stein in my life if I couldn't see him every day in school. And what about Mary Regan? We were at the beginning of an important friendship. Could it continue if we went to different schools?

My thoughts filled me with gloom and foreboding. I could hear Papa coughing in the next room, even as I fell asleep.

20

I GOT A royal welcome from the kids at school.

"Hi, Debbie…" "Glad you're back…" "Too bad about *The Mikado*…" "Good to see you, Debbie."

Mary topped the morning for me. She hugged me and then stepped back to look at my hair.

"You finally did it. It looks great."

"I got my mother in a weak moment. She admitted she liked the way you looked."

"You'll love the freedom it gives you." She tossed her head. "By the way, my Aunt Irene has been asking about you."

"Tell her I've put the fan in a safe place."

"She told me she just knows you'll have an opportunity to use it someday."

"Thank her for me."

I kept looking for Ben. I was dying to meet him face to face and get his reaction to my new look. I saw everybody but Ben, and even ran into Jenny, who put her arms around me.

"I hope you believe me when I tell you I'm glad to see you. Debbie, I've been so worried about that accident in the gym." The sincerity in those green eyes couldn't be doubted. When I told her the truth, she looked relieved.

That was my good deed for the day, I thought, as I continued to look for Ben. If he was in school today, I was sure to find him in Glee Club. On the way there, I stopped to fluff my hair in the girls' room.

Two girls were washing their hands and talking. I didn't listen to them until I heard the name Ben Stein.

"Liz, isn't he the smoothest thing around here?" asked the girl with the bad skin. "A real Rudolph Valentino type, right?"

"He sure is, but there's no use setting your cap for him. I hear the blonde girl with the braids is dating him."

Gossip — that's all it was, but it knocked the air out of me. I was kind of dragging my feet when I opened the door to the classroom and got the surprise of my life.

The whole class stood up to greet me, and clapped their welcome. Miss Beck shook my hand and told me how glad she was to see me. And there was Ben standing in front of me.

"Am I glad to see you! You look different," he said.

"It's a new hair bob. Do you like it?"

"You bet." His dark eyes glowed.

"All right, class. In honor of Deborah's return, we will sing songs from *The Mikado*," Miss Beck announced.

Everyone sang with great spirit and when I got through my solo, unpracticed for three weeks, they were kind in their applause. For once the bell rang too soon. Outside in the yard, a few of us decided to continue at the ice cream parlor.

Not everybody could come. Jenny had a dentist's appointment and Iz had to be someplace, but the trees were in full bloom and the air smelled fresh and green. It was exciting to walk next to Ben.

Seven of us crowded together at one table, so I was pushed quite close to Ben, which I didn't mind at all. Since I was going to be Ben's guest, I ordered a banana split.

"Debbie, you haven't told us yet what school you're attending in the fall," Rose Grau said.

"Jefferson High." I hoped my parents would agree.

"Well, that makes it unanimous at this table," Ben said. Here I was, an accepted member of an important club.

"Have you decided whether you're getting a graduation ring or a pin?"

I hadn't thought about it, and when my banana split arrived in a long dish heaped with scoops of ice cream and topped with syrup, whipped cream, and nuts, I didn't want to.

"Probably a ring," I answered, my mouth full of heavenly tastes. At that moment anything seemed possible.

"How's the ice cream?"

"I love it."

"Don't waste your love on ice cream," Ben said and laughed.

Rose Grau invited all of us to her house Saturday for a party.

"Shall I pick you up for the shindig?" Ben asked.

"Oh, yes, Ben."

Rose mentioned that it would be a party with "you-know-what." I didn't have the foggiest notion what she meant and I didn't care. I was more concerned with what I would wear.

Too bad it was too warm for my new coat. But my new hand-me-down orange crepe dress from Mrs. Fein only needed a hem.

Despite a cheerful welcome from Mr. Desser at my singing lesson on Saturday, my mind was on the party that night. In the middle of my pleasant daydream I forgot where I was.

Mr. Desser tapped my hand. "Debbie, a little attention please! Gone almost a month and you forget everything. Concentrate!"

The session went better after that. At the door, Mr. Desser handed me a letter from Aunt Becky. While I waited for the trolley car I read the short note:

My dear Debbie,
I know you understand why I made this very difficult choice, but you must also believe how sorry I am to lose the love of my family. Perhaps sometime we will meet again. I miss my favorite niece.

Love, Aunt Becky

Her address was included and I promised myself I would find a way to go see her.

My good-as-new dress must have looked fine, because when Ben came that evening he let out a small whistle. After a brief hello to my family, we were off. Papa sat at the table hunched in a heavy sweater, trying not to cough.

Rose Grau lived near Mary Regan, so I knew what kind of house to expect. The party was in full swing when we got there. The gramophone was blaring a foxtrot and everybody was dancing. Jenny Sharp came by, wearing a white dress, held tightly by her partner, Bud Rogers.

A gang of kids was hanging around the punch bowl. "Is it spiked?" Ben asked as he filled two cups.

"Of course not. Mr. and Mrs. Grau don't think we're old enough," said Jack Ross. "And don't forget the Eighteenth Amendment — good old Prohibition, you know."

I didn't know what the complaint was about since the drink was cool and refreshing. We stepped onto the dance floor and joined the other couples. Jane Simmons was at the piano, playing "Baby Face." Ben sang along softly as we danced, and when he reached "You are the cutest little baby face," he gave me a little squeeze. I wanted to go on dancing with him forever, but Rose called out, "Time for games!"

We all crowded into another room, smaller and darker. We played Spin the Bottle and Post Office, and I ended up kissing half the boys in the party. It was fun only when Ben was my partner.

Then there was more dancing. On the dance floor, someone held out a silver flask. "Have some, Ben." He took a swig, shut his eyes for a moment, and held the flask out to me.

I shook my head, but he kept urging, "Go on, try a small one."

A few couples had stopped and were watching me. I put the bottle to my mouth and let a small amount of whiskey trickle in. It tasted horrible. I couldn't help spluttering and coughing as the liquid fire rolled down my throat.

"Another one?"

"No." The others were taking more than one gulp. And when Jenny waltzed by, it was clear she'd had more than one.

"Ben," she said, "didn't you promise me one little dance?"

Ben looked at me. What could I do but nod? Bud Rodgers asked me for a dance. And then it was Jack Ross, and then a few other boys. Well, at least I wasn't a wallflower.

Jane started playing "Ain't We Got Fun?" just as I turned to look for Ben. Where was he? And what had happened to Jenny? I found the answer on my way to the bathroom. From a small alcove under the stairs I could hear Jenny giggling and, a second later, Ben's voice.

The evening was finished for me. I passed a room lined with books and saw Iz talking to another boy. I went in and tapped Iz on the shoulder. "Could I see you a moment, please?"

"What's the matter, Debbie?"

"I've got a headache and I'd like to go home." He was too polite to ask about Ben.

I said good night to Rose Grau, who didn't seem to notice I was leaving with a different boy.

The cool, dark air was soothing. We didn't say much until we had crossed the bridge. Iz was telling me about some scientist he'd just read about, but I wasn't listening. I was hurt by what Ben had done and couldn't take my mind off it. Iz was so excited about the new discovery that he finally drew me into the conversation.

"I'll have to read about him," I promised when we reached my house. "Iz, I want to thank you for being such a good friend."

If I knew nothing else, I knew that Iz Berg, this lanky, sweet guy standing over me, was my friend. And because I thought of him as a friend, I was surprised when he bent down, scooped me up, and planted a kiss full on my mouth.

"I hope you don't mind, Debbie."

I shook my head. The kiss left me dazed and too surprised to say anything.

21

AS I DASHED UP the stairs, I couldn't help thinking it should have been Ben kissing me. I just wanted to get into bed and have a cry with the pillow over my head. Davy was sitting at the kitchen table, and I could hear low voices coming from my parents' bedroom.

"What's going on?"

"Dr. Ferber is here. It's Papa."

Papa had been home for a few days with a hacking cough, and Mama had tried her usual remedies before calling the doctor. She made mustard plasters to apply to his chest and insisted Papa drink large glasses of hot tea loaded with lemon and honey. She had already called Mr. Waldo, the barber, to do cupping. Mama had great faith in Mr. Waldo; he came while Mama was shopping, so I was asked to help.

First, he took out several thick glass cups without handles and placed them on a tray. After pouring alcohol in a basin and lighting a little torch, he asked me to pull up the top of Papa's pajamas and hold it up. Now he had to work quickly.

With one motion, he dipped the glass into the alcohol, applied the torch, and plopped the flaming cup onto Papa's back. After a few minutes, Mr. Waldo pulled off the cup. It left a brown circle where the cup had been — proof, Mama believed, that the bad blood had been drawn out. For a few days, Papa's back would have rows of circles.

Evidently it hadn't worked this time. Papa continued to

have a high fever, so on Sunday Mama finally called Dr. Ferber.

The doctor's face looked serious when he walked into the kitchen with Mama following. I held a clean towel for him while he washed his hands at the kitchen sink.

"Your husband is sick, Mrs. Gold, very sick." Dr. Ferber looked tired. "I am afraid it's pneumonia."

Mama's hands were clutched under her apron. "What has to be done, Doctor?"

"He needs constant care — maybe the hospital."

Mama shook her head. "No hospital, Doctor. We'll give him all the care he needs at home."

"He must be watched day and night, Mrs. Gold."

Mama nodded.

"It may be four or five days before the crisis," Dr. Ferber warned. He gave instructions about medicine and nursing care before he left.

Crisis? The dictionary said it was a turning point, for better or worse. We understood the better and didn't allow ourselves to think about the worse. But it hung in the house like smoke and filled our minds and our lives, as if nothing else existed.

To take care of Papa twenty-four hours a day, we set up a routine. First, the twins and Donny were bundled off to Aunt Rosie's for the duration. Mama was on night watch from midnight until Aunt Sadie arrived about ten in the morning, and then Mama slept. I took over as soon as I got home from school. Mama cooked and cleaned then. David relieved me after supper, staying on until midnight, when Mama came back on duty.

Mrs. Fein and the other neighbors stopped in often during the day to see if we needed anything.

The first day I didn't go to school. I was happy not to have to confront Ben, but by Tuesday I was back. In Glee Club, I buried my head in a book as soon as I sat down. I pretended I didn't hear Ben sit down next to me. If only Miss Beck would sound the chord. No such luck.

"Debbie," Ben's voice was soft. "I want to talk to you."

"About what?"

"I owe you an explanation for Saturday."

"You owe me nothing." I hoped my voice sounded cold.

"But..." I was glad to hear Miss Beck's chord.

At three I hurried out, and although I knew Ben was following me, I didn't turn around. He caught up to me at the gate.

"May I just talk to you for a minute, please?"

I shook my head. "My father is very ill. I have to get home."

"I'm sorry about your father. About Saturday, I want to tell you..."

"I don't want to hear it." I turned to go.

He grabbed my wrist. "Just give me a minute, please!" I stood still and rubbed my wrist.

"First, I want to apologize. I know what I did was inexcusable."

I had nothing to say.

"I...I had too much to drink. Can you forgive me?"

"What difference does it make?" I shrugged my shoulders. "I must get home."

"Not before you tell me you've forgiven me."

"It's all right. I've already forgotten about it," I lied.

He took my hand. "Thanks," he said softly.

I walked quickly to make up for the lost time. My feelings about Ben were in limbo, and I wanted to leave them there. Papa was in my thoughts now. If only Papa would get better.

By Friday morning, Papa's temperature had still not come down. But the crisis had to happen that day. What if it'd happened while I was in school? I ran all the way home. It was quiet in the kitchen — only the clock's ticking could be heard. In the bedroom, Mama was bending over the bed.

"How is he?"

Mama shook her head. Her face was drawn and dark circles lined her eyes. "Aunt Sadie couldn't come today."

"Then you haven't slept at all?"

"I am going to sleep a little now. Watch him. Call me if you need me for anything." She walked wearily out of the room.

Papa was breathing heavily, his face flushed, a blue vein beating over his right eye. I picked up a cool washcloth and patted his hot forehead. He didn't even open his eyes.

I sat by the bed and found myself praying, over and over. When it was time to give Papa his medicine, I called softly, "Papa."

There was no response. I was assured by the beating of the blue vein. "Papa. Papa." The eyes he opened were glazed.

"It's time for your medicine." I supported his head with one hand and offered him the spoon of brown liquid. He drank some water and sank back into his pillow, exhausted.

"Debbie." It was a hoarse whisper.

"What is it?"

I leaned closer to catch what he was saying.

"Get Becky. I want to see Becky."

"Aunt Becky! Why?"

He was already asleep — a deep, noisy sleep.

There was a cold lump of lead in my stomach as I hurried to wake Mama. She was fast asleep on the twins' bed, a cover pulled over her shoulder. A snore was coming from her open mouth.

"Mama." Mama woke with a start. "What? What is it?"

"Papa asked to see Aunt Becky."

Mama's hand flew to her face. I knew at once what was going through her mind — Papa thought he was dying and wanted to see his favorite sister-in-law once more.

"How can we find Becky?" Mama cried.

I was so happy to be able to tell her about the note Mr. Desser had given me.

"Go now. Quickly. Get Becky for Papa."

Mama gave me carfare and I ran to the trolley. It was almost dark when I boarded the second trolley that would take me a few blocks from Aunt Becky's home.

I tried looking out of the window, but I couldn't concentrate. What if Papa died? I tried to run away from that thought, but I could no longer block it out. Death was something that happened to other families, not to my father.

The heavy trolley car wheels seemed to groan, "What if Papa died? What if Papa died?"

The conductor called my stop and I stepped off the trolley into a blinding rain. Tears and raindrops streamed down my face, and I couldn't stop either. An elderly man, walking with his umbrella, stopped to ask if he could help me.

I took a deep breath. "Could you tell me how to get to this address please?"

"Step under my umbrella, little lady." After he studied the address, he said, "It's two blocks from here. Shall I walk you?"

"No, thank you. I'm going to run." I couldn't control my tears as I half ran, half walked. When I reached the right block, I made a pact with God. "Please help my father to get well. And I promise to do a very special good deed."

A sharp bolt of lightning opened the sky as I knocked on the door of a ground-floor apartment of a brownstone house that went up four stories. I stood there trembling, hoping it was the right place. And then, unbelievably, Aunt Becky was standing in the doorway, the light from the room framing her in a soft glow.

"Debbie? Debbie, is it really you?"

I couldn't talk. I just fell into her open arms.

"Am I glad to see you! You're soaking wet, Debbie. Is something wrong?"

"It's Papa."

"Max! What happened?"

She made me take off my wet clothing while I told her about Papa. She gave me her warm robe and a cup of hot tea with lemon and sugar. I stopped shivering.

"Debbie, your clothes are soaked. I couldn't even press them dry because they are dripping." Aunt Becky looked worried. "We don't need two sick people. I think you ought to wait here until John gets home. By then, your things will be dry. You can bring John back with you. Is it all right if I leave right now?"

I nodded, grateful to Aunt Becky for making me see I had to stay put in this small, warm apartment. I was exhausted, but before settling into the armchair by the fireplace, I looked around.

A green rug with bright pink roses covered the living room floor. A small couch in dark green material was facing me. Some of Aunt Becky's favorite mementos stood on the mantelpiece above the fireplace. There I saw the little grass basket I had given her on her birthday.

The kitchen was tiny, and the bedroom was just big enough to hold a large double bed with a brass headboard and a dresser. I studied the pictures on display — John and Becky on their honeymoon and some old shots of the family. I must have been about six when the picture was taken. How young Mama and Papa looked.

I poured another cup of tea and settled into the deep armchair. I must have dozed off. The next thing I was aware of was the sound of a key in the door and the startled face of John O'Neill.

"Debbie, what a lovely surprise." He hugged me. "Becky must be so delighted. Where is Becky?"

I explained and his face grew serious. "Oh, Debbie, I'm so sorry. I'll grab a bite while you're dressing and then we'll be off."

The stars were out and I sniffed the rain-washed streets. The night seemed so clear and peaceful. But what about Papa? Had he gotten through the crisis or…I shuddered.

"Cold, Debbie?" Uncle John put his arm through mine. On the trolley car, he told me about their honeymoon to Niagara Falls.

"It sounds like fun, and a wonderful place to see."

"Great for honeymoons."

It wasn't until we were standing in front of my house that I remembered John had never been in our home, had never met the family, and perhaps would not be welcomed. What should I do? I wanted desperately to run inside, but John...

He must have sensed my embarrassment. "Debbie, I'll have a smoke and wait down here. Just tell Becky where I am."

I vaulted up the stairs and then stopped at the door, too scared to open it. I grasped the doorknob and inched the door open. Everybody was home.

"Papa," I gasped. "How is Papa?"

"He's not sick any more," Michael said, dancing a little circle.

"That's right," Elliot chimed in.

I swooped the baby off the floor and covered him with joyful kisses. If his little neck got wet, this sweet baby wouldn't know that some tears got mixed in with the kisses.

Aunt Becky and Mama walked into the kitchen, the weariness magically gone from Mama's face.

"Where's John?" Becky asked.

"Downstairs, waiting for you."

"You left Becky's husband downstairs?" Mama asked. "Shame, Debbie. Bring him right up. What is he going to think of us?"

The radiant look on Aunt Becky's face almost made me cry again. Her family was finally going to meet John. I went down slowly to give Mama a chance to wash her face and put on a clean apron.

Papa always said that we must make something good from the bad. Had he planned this somehow?

When I returned, holding John by the hand, my family was waiting to meet him. Aunt Becky kissed him and then turned shyly for the introductions.

"Molly, this is John, John O'Neill, my husband. Darling, this is my sister, Molly Gold."

We were all stunned when Mama replied, "Pleased I should meet you." It was her first complete sentence in English.

22

PAPA'S RECOVERY was slow. Even though he tired easily, he was chafing to return to work. When Dr. Ferber suggested he needed to rest in the country, Papa laughed.

"You don't understand, Dr. Ferber. I have a son who is going to college and a daughter who will be at Jefferson High School in the fall. No, Doctor, I have to get back to the shop."

Although money was scarce, I desperately wanted the graduation ring. The bills grew longer in Mr. Pofsky's black "owing book," and I went back to work there.

Waiting on customers wasn't bad since I knew my way around now and recognized the customers by their names. From listening to their conversations I knew who was having a baby and when, how to treat the croup, and other interesting topics that were never taught in school.

Everyone had an opinion about Papa's illness: Go to the country, stay in bed, use hot mustard plasters, get cupping done. When Papa finally regained his strength, he put on the blue suit that now hung so loosely on his thin frame and returned to work.

At the grocer's one day, Mrs. Cohen told me she was worried that her husband was not prepared to take the test to become an American citizen. I told her I'd helped my aunts with their tests, and she asked me if I would tutor her husband. We made an appointment for Sunday.

I agreed to help without even wondering whether I would get paid. As Papa said, "Sometimes a person should do a favor without thinking of getting paid."

The citizenship test wasn't easy. I'd seen how my aunts and uncles had to struggle to learn everything.

On Sunday I walked to the Cohens' apartment and met Mr. Cohen, a short, nervous man with strong opinions. He didn't know that women now had the right to vote. He didn't believe in that, he said. But of course I didn't agree with him.

I brought with me the book Aunt Becky had used in preparing for her citizenship test. In the next hour I went over with Mr. Cohen some of the information he would need to know about the government of the United States.

Mr. Cohen complimented me on my knowledge. He told me that if he passed, he wanted to give me a gift. "And, Debbie, I have some friends who could use such a good teacher. I'm going to recommend you."

"Wow," I thought as I walked home, "maybe I'll be a teacher."

School was easier as graduation approached because I knew my parents would let me go to Jefferson. Two groups had formed in the graduating class. Those who planned to continue school looked down on the others who were going to work.

Despite my loyalty to Esther, I was drawn to the snobby ones, who spent most of their time talking about what high school would be like. Everybody except me was sporting a graduation ring.

"Aren't you getting a ring, Debbie?" Jenny asked.

"Of course, I am," I said, not wanting to give her a chance to hurt me again. But there was no way I could afford the ring. With Papa just back to work and all those bills, I didn't have the heart to ask for the money.

That evening Mr. Cohen came to the house, very excited and happy.

"You are looking at an American citizen, Debbie." After I introduced him to my family, he told them what a good teacher I was. Then he gave me an envelope.

"I promised you a present. And here are the addresses of two men who work in my shop. Thanks again, Debbie."

When he left I opened the envelope. It was a five-dollar bill! Maybe I could buy the ring after all. If the other two men from Mr. Cohen's shop would give me the same, I'd have just enough.

I looked at my parents. "Do you think you could loan me the rest so I would have fifteen dollars to buy the ring this week? Then I'll pay you back from my tutoring."

Papa looked at Mama and when she nodded he said, "We'll lend you some of the rent money."

I got the ring and was able to pay back the money before the rent was due. Ben and I were seeing more of each other than ever. Only Papa worried me.

One night his coughing was so bad it woke me up. I remembered I'd promised to perform a good deed if Papa got through the pneumonia crisis. I decided to act on that promise the very next day.

Of all the people I knew, Eddie Pofsky needed help the most. Always alone, he spent his days in the back apartment or sitting in front of the grocery store. When he went for a walk, kids often threw rocks at him.

A trip to the ocean would be just the thing for him. At breakfast I asked the twins if they'd like to come with us.

"With Loony Eddie? Where did you want to go with him?" was Michael's reply.

"I thought we'd go to Coney Island. I'm sure he'd enjoy the beach and the boardwalk. Wouldn't you?"

"Yeah, but not with him."

"How about you, Elliot?"

Elliot shrugged his shoulders. He was still letting Michael speak for him. There'd be no help from my brothers, so when I saw Iz at school I told him my plan.

"If you like I'll come along and invite my sister, Sarah, too," he said.

"That's perfect, Iz."

The Pofskys were delighted with my plans for the outing.

"Debbie, do you really want to give up a Sunday for Eddie?" Mrs. Pofsky asked. I thought I saw tears in her eyes as she turned to take care of a customer.

When I told Eddie, he clapped his hands and rolled his head, his small, blue eyes lighting up with joy.

It was a perfect May morning when Iz, Sarah, and I walked to the Pofskys' to pick up Eddie. He was ready in his brown knickers, tan sweater, and tan cap. Mrs. Pofsky tucked some clean, white handkerchiefs in Eddie's pockets and gave me a few extras. Iz picked up the picnic basket the Pofskys had insisted on filling for us and we were off.

I talked with Sarah as we rode on the two trolley cars to Coney Island. Although she was only ten, she was an avid reader, and we talked about some of our favorite books. When I told her I, too, had a big brother, we compared notes, and I knew I had a real friend.

The very first moment Eddie saw Iz he clung to him. From their seat on the trolley car, I could hear Eddie's giggling and see Iz using the handkerchiefs.

At the beach, we took off our shoes and socks and waded into the ocean holding hands. We had fun watching Eddie's terror turn to delight when a wave swirled around our ankles. We built sand castles, collected shells, and splashed in the water. Soon we were starving, and we dived into the delicious food in the basket.

At the bottom of the bag of cookies we found an envelope marked, "For the boardwalk." There was enough money for some treats and a ride or two. We cleaned up quickly, anxious to get to the boardwalk. Sarah and I, arm in arm, followed Iz and Eddie.

"Let's try the Ferris wheel first," Iz called back. "Okay, Eddie?"

When we got to the big wheel and Eddie saw how high it went up, he shook his head.

Iz turned to me and said, "Why don't you and Sarah go up and we'll wave to you?"

Eddie gaped and waved at us until our car stopped at the top of the Ferris wheel. Then he had to hide his eyes. But the merry-go-round was perfect for Eddie, so we all enjoyed it.

"Let's get some food," Sarah suggested. We walked the whole length of the boardwalk trying to decide what to buy. It was hard to choose between the hot dogs, the *knishes*, the french-fried potatoes, and all the ices and ice creams.

But finally, after we'd worked up a real appetite, we bought four hot dogs. The mustard and hot sauerkraut made them taste so good we just had to lick our fingers. And there was enough money left to share two cones of cotton candy.

Eddie, unused to so much activity, fell fast asleep on the way home. Iz hoisted him to his shoulder and carried him the three blocks from the trolley to the Pofskys'.

While Mrs. Pofsky was putting Eddie to bed, the rest of us sat in their big room and talked.

"I'd like to see Eddie again, Mr. Pofsky," Iz said. "On Sundays, when the store is closed, could you use somebody to sweep, stock the shelves, wash the counter, and whatever?"

Mr. Pofsky smiled. "With my arthritis, I really do need somebody. Are you willing to work? Of course, we'll have to agree on what to pay you."

Iz nodded. "Besides Debbie reading to him, I think I can teach Eddie something if I let him be my assistant."

He asked Mrs. Pofsky to sew two aprons with deep pockets. Into each apron Iz put dust rags, washcloths, scouring powder, a bar of yellow soap, a hammer, and nails.

On Sundays, Eddie followed Iz around the store, proudly wearing his apron. He delighted in following Iz's orders.

"Got a hammer, Eddie?"

"Hand me the yellow soap."

"Find your dust rag and clean this shelf."

And one Sunday I heard Iz say, "Find your handkerchief, Eddie. Wipe your mouth."

23

PAPA'S COUGHING still woke me up at night and made me question the good deed I'd promised to do. All I really did for Eddie was arrange the outing, because from the moment Iz had walked into the grocery, Eddie had never let go of him.

Iz had done everything to take care of Eddie, while Sarah and I just had fun. So had I really done a good deed?

I asked Mama if going to see old Mrs. Oliver, my hospital roommate, was considered a good deed.

"Yes, it's a *mitzvah*, Debbie," she said. I decided to take some cookies to Mrs. Oliver, who was now living at the Home for the Aged.

Esther couldn't come with me, so I asked Ben. He agreed only after I told him how nervous I was about the visit. When we entered the somber, gray building and were admitted by the stern-faced matron, I was really glad he was with me.

Mrs. Oliver's eyes brightened when she saw us. She insisted on taking us around the dayroom to be introduced.

As we passed a dusty piano, Ben banged out a few notes, which caused an instant commotion in the large room. Many of the elderly residents who were nodding in their chairs woke up. Several moved toward the piano in their wheelchairs, or came hobbling on canes.

"Can you play?..." "Our piano player died last year..." "That was six months ago, Livy... " "Play for us, play anything, please."

I didn't have any music with me, but Ben suggested we sing some songs from *The Mikado*. At first, our voices sounded flat in the large room, but the audience soon warmed us up with their hand clapping, foot tapping, cane stamping, and their calls for "More! More!"

The ruckus brought the stern-faced matron running. When she realized what was happening she smiled.

And then Ben was saying maybe we could perform *The Mikado* here. Was he serious?

The old people must have heard us, because we could hear them whispering. A murmur of "*Mikado...The Mikado*" ran through the room.

"There's no stage, and the piano's out of tune," I pointed out.

The matron said thoughtfully that the piano could be tuned. And couldn't that corner of the room be partitioned off for a stage? Ben and I looked at each other and promised to ask Miss Beck and the rest of the cast.

When we asked the other kids, they almost unanimously approved the idea, and Miss Beck agreed to play piano. Mr. Davis gave us permission and reminded us to get consent letters from our parents. In parting, he said he just might come to the performance.

The next week, the kids descended upon the nursing home every day to prepare the set and rehearse. The cooperation between the cast and the elderly residents was fantastic.

Mrs. Oliver put herself in charge of the cleaning squad. The slight lady with the cane was everywhere, giving orders, handing out cleaning materials, inspecting work. Some of the old folks grumbled, but one woman, polishing a small table beside her wheelchair, remarked, "I'd forgotten how good it feels to work!"

Unexpected help came from many sources. Ben persuaded his uncle who was a piano tuner to work on the old piano. Some parents donated sheets for a curtain and others sewed them.

Iz was in charge of building the makeshift stage, and he

seemed to be all over the place. He quickly learned the names of most of the old people and became their favorite. He sometimes discussed their health with them and soon was being called "Dr. Iz."

Sometimes when I looked at Iz, I was filled with wonder at his energy and kindness. But when I looked at Ben's handsome face, my heart sang. One afternoon as Esther and I walked home from school, I tried to explain to her the difference between Iz and Ben.

Esther nodded. "I don't have such a problem. Herb's no Valentino, and he's not planning to be a doctor."

Esther had been dating Herb Levy since they had met in Woolworth's one day. When she told him she'd be working there in September, he had said he, too, was going to Continuation School while he worked in a factory.

"In fact," Esther said proudly, "Herb's already completed two years of high school, and the owner of the factory has promised him a good job when he graduates."

Esther sounded so serious that I turned to look at her. "Esther, honestly, you look taller. And have you lost weight?"

"Maybe I have. You see, Herb mentioned once he doesn't like fat women."

"I can't wait to meet him, Es."

"You will, you will."

As I approached home, I was so absorbed in thinking about Esther I'd forgotten Aunt Becky would be there that night. She was holding Donny, and I kissed them both.

"I'm so glad you're having supper with us tonight, Aunt Becky. John is coming later to see *The Mikado*, isn't he?"

"Yes, he's looking forward to it." Aunt Becky looked a little pale, and I thought it was because she was pregnant. Mama had told me the news yesterday.

"Are you feeling okay?" I asked her.

"Yes, I'm fine."

"And where's Mama?" I called, as I walked into the bedroom.

There was no answer. Something was wrong.

"Debbie, sit down," Aunt Becky said when I returned to the kitchen. "There is something I have to tell you. You know your Papa has been coughing a lot lately. He and Mama had to go over to Dr. Ferber's office and he had to take a Board of Health test."

"But he's been coughing for a long time."

"Yes, but now he is coughing up...blood."

"Coughing blood? Is that very bad?"

Aunt Becky clasped her hands. "I'm not sure, but it could be consumption."

I gasped and clamped my hand over my mouth. Consumption was a dreaded illness. People always whispered the word.

"If Papa has...this thing, what will happen to him?" I asked.

"He'll have to go away, to a sanitarium."

I took Donny in my arms and hugged him hard. I didn't know what to do or say, so I handed the baby back to Aunt Becky and went into my bedroom. I was just sitting on the bed, staring, dazed and shocked, when she walked in.

"I can't sing tonight, Aunt Becky. I can't do Yum-Yum, not now." I couldn't hold back my tears.

She took my hand in hers. "Debbie, you are going to have to grow up, especially if your father goes to a sanitarium. It won't help him to see you so upset. Besides, he will probably have to miss your graduation."

"And David's graduation from high school, too?"

"Yes. So think how much he'll enjoy seeing you tonight, starring in *The Mikado*. Now when Mama and Papa come home, if you want to help him feel better, you must be cheerful."

By the time my parents returned, I'd bathed and washed and set my hair. Mama looked exhausted, but Papa seemed himself.

"All ready for tonight, Debbie? I told the men in the shop you were going to sing and they were so excited. I am, too."

I smiled and tried to look into his eyes, but Papa knew I was troubled. "I guess Becky told you that I have to go to the country. I'll be going to a sanitarium in Liberty."

"Yes, Papa."

"It's just for the summer months. By the time you start high school, I'll be home."

I glanced at Mama. She had a blank look in her eyes. I didn't know whether I could believe Papa would be back.

I was glad Iz was walking with me to the performance. I needed to know about this illness, so without telling him about Papa, I asked him if he knew anything about consumption.

"Consumption. The real name is tuberculosis, and it's a poor man's disease. It affects the lungs and usually wastes the body, producing a low-grade fever."

"Iz, you sound like a textbook."

"I've looked it up before. Many people have it."

"Do people...die from it?"

"Sometimes. But fresh air, good food, and lots of rest usually help them recover."

"They go to a sanitarium for that, don't they?"

"Yeah. You sure are asking a lot of gloomy questions tonight, Debbie. I hope nothing's wrong."

I couldn't confide in him, not yet. I didn't want to start crying so I said nothing.

Mrs. Oliver was waiting to help me dress. The kimono she had offered to lend me hung neatly on the door of her bedroom; all the creases had been ironed out of it.

"This kimono will make you the most beautiful Yum-Yum ever." She glowed with pride. I was able to concentrate on my performance until Mrs. Oliver started making up my eyes.

"You would be surprised if I told you that at one time I had stage ambitions myself," she said.

"You are full of surprises, Mrs. Oliver."

She was looking right into my eyes, trying to decide how

to do the make-up. It seemed she could see what was locked up in me. A big sob tore itself from deep inside me, and there was no stopping the tears.

Mrs. Oliver pressed a small handkerchief into my hands. "Debbie, this is just stage nerves." I shook my head. "What is it then?"

I couldn't talk, and the sobs were coming fast.

"Now, Deborah, listen to me." There was quiet authority in her voice. "Take deep breaths. Start right now. Breathe in, let it out, breathe in, breathe out."

Her steady voice helped me stop crying, and I got my breathing back to normal.

"Use this cold water to wash your face, and hold the wet handkerchief over your eyes."

With the cooling handkerchief over my eyes, I was able to pour out the whole story to her. I even used the dreaded word "consumption."

"That is trouble, my dear. Now I understand."

"You don't understand everything. If I don't get to Jefferson High, I won't see Ben Stein anymore."

"Why don't you cross that bridge when you come to it?" she advised. "Now you have to get ready to do the most important thing — make your father proud of you."

"I know. I'm all right now. But my eyes look puffy."

"Don't worry. This make-up will make you look like an authentic Japanese girl." I slipped into the soft kimono, picked up the little fan Aunt Irene had given me, and went to join the rest of the cast. Mrs. Oliver must have been right. When I walked out to join the other kids in their costumes, there were many compliments. The best came from Ben. "So this is what Yum-Yum looks like. She is really beautiful."

I wanted to kiss him and tell him how handsome he looked in his kimono. I couldn't help feeling this might be the last thing we would do together. Would I see Ben if we weren't in the same school in September?

I closed my eyes to brush away all those questions and

concentrate only on tonight. It was going to be a night for Papa to remember.

On the other side of the curtain, Miss Beck was playing the introduction. When she finished, a wave of excitement swept through us as the curtain parted to reveal Nanki-Poo carrying a guitar over his shoulder. There was loud applause from the audience, and the play began.

I peeked through the curtains and spotted Papa and Mama, looking so good together. Aunt Becky and Uncle John sat beside them.

And then it was my cue, and a miracle happened. I was no longer Deborah Gold—I was a beautiful Japanese girl in love with a handsome young troubador, but sad because I was betrothed to an old man.

I kept from looking at Mama and Papa until my solo, the "Moon Song." Then one quick glance was enough. I could see Papa's pride on his beaming face.

Afterwards, the applause from the elderly residents and our parents was deafening. What a sweet sound clapping hands make! The audience wouldn't let us go, and Miss Beck directed us to repeat one of the shorter songs.

Someone handed me a bouquet of roses. It was from my family, and as I left the stage, I blew a kiss to my proud parents.

I was happy I could give Papa that night. Three days later he was off to the sanitarium in Liberty. Now we were faced with the grim reality of having to survive without Papa.

24

Mama, always frugal, was more so now. She made meals out of bones and leftovers. My aunts helped out by bringing cooked dishes from time to time.

Even Uncle Pincus had made a generous gesture before Papa left. "Don't worry about the money you owe me, Max. When I get it back is soon enough." And then he had proposed, "After Debbie gets her working papers, I'll give her a job in my factory. And Davy can work for me while he's going to college."

"Thanks, Pincus," Papa said. "I'll be back in September, and both David and Debbie will be going to school."

"How much education does a girl need anyhow?" Uncle Pincus grumbled. Although Mama's eyes flashed up at him, neither she nor my father said anything.

So I answered, "As much as she can get."

I knew I'd do anything rather than work in Uncle Pincus's factory. Through the summer I prayed every day that Papa would get well and come home, and that I could go to Jefferson High School.

Mary and I received honorable mention for our Patrick Henry report at graduation, but without Papa, there was little pleasure in it for me.

Early in July, I got time off from working at Pofsky's to spend a day at Coney Island with the cast of *The Mikado*. Wearing bathing suits under our clothes and carrying packed lunches, we were a jolly, singing group as we rode the open trolleys to the beach.

I swam and sunned with Ben, trying to pretend everything was wonderful. At the end of the afternoon I told him about Papa.

"You mean you won't be going to Jefferson in September?" He sat up to look at me.

"That's right."

"Gee, that's tough." He was upset and didn't seem to know what to say.

"Of course, my father may get better and be back by September," I said. I had a feeling it wasn't true, because Mama and Dr. Ferber both avoided talking about it. But I hoped that somehow the doctors could be mistaken.

It was the last time I saw Ben all summer. He sent me a card from the Catskills, where his family was spending the summer.

By August we learned that Papa couldn't come home in September. He might be gone for a long time.

At the end of the month, Mama said we'd be moving into the janitor's flat in a big apartment house nearby. In exchange for rent and a small salary, we would clean, tend furnace, sweep sidewalks, haul trash cans, and be at the beck and call of tenants.

I pounded my head into my pillow that night, saying over and over, "Janitor's girl, janitor's girl." I wondered how it would sound to Ben.

At first, the landlord did not want us without Papa, but David convinced him that, except for Donny, each of us would do a share of the work. I would have my own bedroom at last, a very small room, but with Aunt Becky's promise of a bedspread, at least a glimmer of excitement.

On moving day, there was a sad echo in our empty flat as Mama said good-bye to her friends and I stacked dishes in a deep barrel for moving. David and Iz helped Tony, our iceman, load the furniture into his horse-drawn wagon. He had already delivered one load.

The kitchen felt dismal. Without Mama's starched curtains, the windows looked naked. I noticed for the first time the brown, worn spots on the linoleum that I'd scrubbed so faithfully every Friday. Tears slid down my face as I wrapped and packed the dishes.

I heard footsteps on the stairs, and Iz came in. "Everything ready for the second load?"

I turned away so he would not see me crying. "Just a minute," I mumbled.

I grabbed the last dishes and loaded them into the barrel. In my haste, I forgot about the nail sticking out from the barrel.

"Ouch!" I put my finger into my mouth.

"Let me see," Iz said, checking the nail in the barrel. "It's a rusty nail, and I think we'd better get the finger bleeding." He squeezed it hard. "That's better. Hey, am I hurting you?" he asked when he saw my tears.

"Just a reaction, I guess. But thanks, Iz, you really are a good friend."

I meant that. Since Papa had left, Iz had been at our house often, although I was never sure whom he was visiting. The twins were certain he came to play the harmonica for them. When David was around, they discussed crystal sets and radios. Mama thought Iz came to praise her cooking.

It didn't matter that Iz had seen me with my hair mussed so many times. I'd gotten used to his funny face and his kind ways.

"Only a good friend, Deb?" We were sitting close, my bandaged finger resting in his big hand. What did he mean? I said nothing.

Iz placed my hand on my lap. Then he leaned over and put his two hands around my face. Why, he's going to kiss me, I thought, and closed my eyes.

The next few moments took me completely by surprise. Iz was pressing his mouth against mine, and I was responding and eagerly kissing him back. What was happening? My head seemed to be spinning in the stars.

138

When I opened my eyes, Iz was looking at me. There was a glow about him. Why hadn't I ever noticed the beauty and dignity of his face?

I started to tell Iz what was happening, but Tony and David came in just then. Iz looked intently at me for a moment, then went to help the others. Before he left, Davy dropped a letter in my lap.

While they carried things downstairs, I thought about this new way of seeing Iz. Ben, so popular, so good-looking, had kissed me many times, but there had been no stars. And now Iz, who wasn't my ideal at all, but somehow... Love was sure a mystery, and I was going to find out more about it. Maybe that's what growing up was all about.

I opened the letter David had left. It was from Mr. Desser. I had told him last week that I wouldn't be able to continue with my lessons for a while because of Papa.

"You won't give up, Debbie?" he had asked.

"No, of course not, just until things settle down."

He had actually kissed the top of my head before I left. Then he removed his glasses and cleaned them with his white handkerchief.

Mama came in while I was reading his letter. "Mama, Mr. Desser says the Settlement House is giving me a scholarship so I can continue my voice lessons. He doesn't think I should take a vacation from learning to sing properly."

"Debbie, that's good." Mama nodded her approval. "But now, Debbile, I have to talk to you."

Mama hardly ever called me "Debbile," so what was she going to say? That David should go to college in September?

As much as I wanted to go to Jefferson High, if there had to be a choice between us, Davy should be the one to go to school. I only hoped we could afford it.

Mama was leaning against the icebox. The late sun sent a shaft of light through the uncurtained windows. There were lines on her face and gray in her hair, but her eyes were shining as if she'd seen a vision.

"You know, when I was in Europe, everybody always used

to say that in America, there are streets of gold. The streets are paved with gold, I heard so many times. America, the golden land. I couldn't wait to come to this country." She laughed.

"When I got here, where was the gold? Everything was filthy. Every day I worked in a dirty loft, and every night I came home to a room I shared with others on the fifth floor of a cold-water flat. My bed was a mattress on the floor. I earned next to nothing."

Mama had a strange expression on her face. Was she all right?

"Then I met Papa and got married. I remember I asked Papa if he knew about the gold. He didn't know either."

Mama smiled. "But now, all of a sudden, after all these years, I know where the gold in America is." Her voice was high-pitched and excited. She faced me, but her eyes were focused somewhere in the distance.

"You know where the gold is, Mama?"

"Debbile, listen carefully. The gold, the gold is in the opportunity America gives everybody to get an education." Now Mama was looking at me. "So here is what we must do. That little bedroom that you were supposed to get..."

"Mama, you mean my own little room that I was going to have for the first time in my life?"

She went on as if I had not interrupted. "That little bedroom we are going to rent to Mrs. Fein's cousin. He just came to America and needs a place to live. You understand, Debbie?"

What could I say? I nodded. "But, Mama, maybe I could put a bed in the front hallway. I'd have some privacy that way. Or maybe it would be better if I moved into your bedroom?"

Mama shook her head. "No. And Donny won't sleep with me either. He'll be with Davy in your big bed. You'll use David's cot..."

"But your bedroom..."

Mama held her hand up. "Mrs. Cohen's sister just lost her

husband, and she has to go to work. She needs a place to live, where someone can take care of her four-year-old daughter."

"You mean..."

"That's right. She will have my room."

I couldn't keep up and my head was reeling. "Mama, where will you sleep?"

"Sleep? I'll sleep on chairs, on a feather quilt, wherever there's room. Does it make a difference where you sleep?"

"No, Mama. I guess not. But I don't understand...."

"Mrs. Fein's cousin and Mrs. Cohen's sister will pay us room and board from their wages. In this way, we can send David to college."

Now I understood. But Mama had more to say.

"And you — you must go to high school."

"Mama, do you mean that?"

She nodded. "It will be hard work. But when Davy finishes college, I think he will be able to help you for the next four years."

"College for me?"

Mama continued with her dream. "When Michael and Elliot are ready, the two of you can help them. And Donny..."

Now I could see the vision Mama saw. "I know, Mama! We'll all help Donny."

I was stunned. For the first time, I realized how much Mama wanted for all of us. She was no greenhorn. She understood America and its streets of gold.

I wanted to cry and hug my mother. But when I looked up, her everyday face was back.

I could hear Tony, David, and Iz outside, waiting for us. Mama picked up the last small box of our belongings and walked to the door.

I draped the few remaining clothes over my arm and took a last look at the empty rooms. Then I left for my new home and my new life, following in Mama's firm footsteps.

Glossary

Ach Dumkopf! "Oh, dummy!"

Bar Mitzvah (Hebrew) The ceremony for a thirteen-year-old Jewish boy that marks his reaching the status of a man; usually held in a temple or synagogue.

Baruch Atah (Hebrew) "Blessed art Thou"; the opening words of a prayer.

Bintel Brief An advice column in a Jewish newspaper.

Blintz A crepe-like pancake filled with cheese, fruit, or vegetables; rolled and sauteed in butter until golden brown.

Borsht A soup made from beets, served with a boiled potato, and topped with a dollop of sour cream.

Challa A braided loaf of white bread made with eggs, soft to the touch and delicate in flavor; served at the Sabbath dinner.

Charoses A mixture of chopped nuts, apples, cinnamon, and wine eaten as part of the Seder ritual; symbolic of the mortar made by the Israelites in slavery, with the sweetness representing the hope of freedom.

Dayenu (Hebrew) "It would have sufficed"; a song for the Passover **Seder**.

Gefilte fish Finely chopped fish, such as pike, carp, or whitefish, mixed with matzo meal, eggs, and seasonings, shaped into patties, and simmered in vegetable broth until done.

Greenhorn   A recent immigrant; especially one who is unaware or ignorant of American ways.

Gut, Gut!   "Good, Good!"

Gut Shabbes   "Good Sabbath"; a greeting that ushers in the Sabbath.

Haggadah (Hebrew)   The narrative used at the Passover **Seder** to relate the story of Israel's bondage in, and flight from, Egypt.

Karpas (Hebrew)   Greens, such as lettuce, cress, or parsley, dipped into salt water and eaten during the Passover **Seder** as a reminder to give thanks for the fruit of the earth.

Keppele   "Little head"; a diminutive or affectionate word for head.

Kiddush (Hebrew)   The blessing over the wine used to hallow the Sabbath and Jewish holy days.

Knish   A little dumpling filled with grated potatoes, cheese, or groats.

Kosher   Ritually prepared according to Jewish dietary laws; therefore fit to eat.

Latke   A pancake made from raw grated potatoes.

Maror (Hebrew)   A bitter herb, such as horseradish, eaten during the Passover **Seder** as a reminder of the bitterness of the slavery of the Israelites in Egypt.

Matzo   Unleavened bread; traditionally eaten during Passover.

Meshugge   Crazy, insane, or absurd.

Mitzvah   A good work; a kind, considerate, ethical deed.

Musiker   A musician; especially an accomplished one.

Nosh   A tidbit or snack.

Oy gevalt!   "Oh, help!"; a cry of fear, dismay, or alarm.

Pishke   A little can, used to collect money for charity; often kept in the kitchen.

Pogrom   An organized massacre of a minority group of people; usually a massacre of Jews.

Ruggele A sweet pastry filled with fruit, nuts, and sugar and rolled to form a crescent.

Schlimazel A born loser, for whom nothing goes right: when he sells rainwear, the sun comes out.

Seder The ritual Passover feast that retells the story of Exodus in prayers, biblical stories, and songs.

Shivah A week of mourning for the dead.

Shtarke A strong person.

Shtetl A small town in Eastern Europe where Jews lived in close community.

Strudel A pastry made from dough stretched and rolled into many, paper-thin layers, filled with fruit or cheese, brushed heavily with butter, and baked until crisp; best served warm from the oven.

Tante Aunt.

Tsimmes A dish made with carrots, sweet potatoes, prunes, and sometimes beef.

Yiddish A rich and colorful language spoken by Eastern European Jews; derived mostly from German and Hebrew, but also from Czech, Polish, Russian, Rumanian, Old French, and Old Italian. Yiddish uses the Hebrew alphabet and is written from right to left.